OF LIFE AND TIME,
THAT NOW AND THEN RHYME

Stories, Poems, and Pieces

MARK RANEY

ISBN: 978-0-578-02854-5

To Valerie and Ray for four minute eggs on toast long ago, and so much more.

TABLE OF CONTENTS

THE MERRY GO ROUND

It is a merry go round and I want to ride it as I watch it go whirling by to the gay whistle music of the steam calliope and most of all I want to ride it too because it is going by fun fast and the stampeding horses are pretty and the laughing riders are silly as I stand breezy near, but I cannot step on so I run along side but I cannot run fast enough to even jump on so there whirling by merrily is the everything that I will ever want but it goes on whirling by and I will never get on.

THE STONE WALL

Spring came warm, and with it baby grass came on the front yard slope we had cleared before the sidewalk then the road. We had gathered many various rocks from open fields around Raleigh that previous fall to build a stone wall in the deep cut we had made in the clay bank that was below the topsoil. It was very hard work, and it took lots of beer to complete. The sidewalk doubters laughed and swore that the stone wall would never stand though. But we began with a sound foundation, we mixed the mortar well, we layed the stones carefully, and we left peephole openings. Our stone wall would stand! So we called ourselves "Lambie Pies" for an unknown reason that shouted pride in Lambda Chi Alpha and in the stone wall in front of our Fraternity House. But we became wolfy as hell when anyone else dared to call us such a silly name. Winters' downpours and freezes passed, spring brought baby grass, and our stone wall stood.

GIRLS

It's funny. You can take the goofiest clod ever, wearing bib overalls with a snuff stick stuck in his mouth, sit him on a Fraternity House porch in summer, and girls will ride by all day and rip their cheeks smiling invitingly, their hair tossing in the warm wind.

SPRING

Spring was in me like it gets into trees and makes them fresh and happy again, until it is difficult to remember the cold times. But cold times have a purpose also. So it is for me to withstand, then I will have both times to enjoy.

WE WERE

We were the swiftest of an age,
and the fittest of an age,
    and laziness was the smile
    we always wore.

We were the most outrageous of an age,
and the most boring of an age,
    and sophistication was the brass ring
    we always prized.

We were the brightest of an age,
and the surest of an age,
    and doubt was the truth
    we always told.

We were the most egotistical of an age,
and the most fickle of an age,
    and selflessness was the handshake
    we always gave.

We were the hope of an age,

and the future of an age,

　　　and greatness was the tomorrow

　　　that we would have.

We were the boldest of an age,

and the bravest of an age,

　　　and recklessness was the toast

　　　we always made.

We were the State College men of an age,

and the Engineers of an age,

　　　and Lambda Chis were what

　　　we would be for life.

And we laughed by day,

and we sang by night,

　　　and love was the flower

　　　we almost held.

THE VOICE FROM THE EAST

In the movement of men, and their quests and their deeds, there is a descriptive tide that surges and wanes and then replenishes itself. Voids are created and needs exist, then time satisfies and allows the filling. But if tide could speak what would she say, and how would she tell her story?

Because it is true that there is a voice from the sea coast, a voice from the low farms there, that is telling of a need and is ringing the call. And the voice from the East is composing now. And the voice from the East is gathering tone and melody and harmony now. And the voice from the East is building intensity now, that reminisces about the past while sounding the future's promises.

The voice from the East is seasoned with fresh water and yellow sand and brine water and white dunes and black ooze. She is tinted with soil and fish and tobacco and corn. Because she is fertilizer and peaches and pine trees and a hard salty wind and a quiet blinding sun. And she will always be crop rows running together in the evening stillnesses' of a time to harvest.

Because the voice from the East recalls very well the loud parade that passed her way. The parade that went from her grand shores on to the Piedmont, then to the high mountains and to the far unknowns that were beyond. She knows that a great many traveled into the sun, that some remained without the journey, and that a few so few returned. So she can well chart her disappointments and her hurts and her sadness's. Because she

7

had sent all these men West for them to see and to learn and to settle. But most of them soon forgot the fine place of their beginning. And most of them soon dismissed the fair home of their first steps. So in the hot sun and the ground fog and the beautiful moon of many lifetimes she waited and she hoped and she watched for a return for any return, for a coming back to build the all that had been so quickly passed. But hundreds of men were born and put into their far rocky earth and thousands of their generations also, and yet so very very few men returned to build the East. So her voice became gradually reduced as its size shrank and as its scale became limited, this while the West grew powerful and big and expensive and mechanical.

But her voice will reduce no more! But her voice will limit no longer! And never again will her voice shrink. Not because of the returns that have not come and may never come. Not because of men who became both fickle and faint, and distracted by a newer and a brighter toy. Because the East has come to know that her real strength is in the men who stayed, yes they always, and in the so few who did return, and in the several who came from other places to take her promise as their promise. So the voice from the East waits no longer and never again, having begun with the very much that she already had. But the East is still quite proud of the West, and prouder still of the State that they share. And now she has begun to build with the same true dedication with which she ushered in the West. Because she too can learn, and she too can see and can settle, because she too can do while doing it better.

So even though there is an imaginary line that divides our State, our two loves are one love, and our two goals are one goal. So others really only see the one face of a solid North Carolina. And this is the way that it should be, and this is the way that it is, after all it is only a within the family matter. But here in the East there is so much to be done, beginning now, and so very far to go. Because the old industries and the old ways will have to be replaced, and a far stronger statue constructed. So, yes, there is work to be done and land to use and many things to concentrate on. But we wait no more! Not for a return that has not come and may never come. Because we too can rise! Because we too can win!

ALL HIS EYES COULD SEE

Ralph's totally confused brain raced at a thousand miles an hour. He sat on the edge of his chair that was pushed away from his cluttered desk. He took several deep breaths and tried to calm down. But with each breath his throat wheezed from too many cigarettes, and this wheezing disturbed him. 'I'm a wreck, I'm a wreck', flashed on his brain in disgust. So he reached to his shirt pocket for a cigarette, his shoulders hunched and his head bowed. The lighter in his pants pocket was under his leg. He groped for it without realizing where it was. Then he stared at it trying to decide what it was. Then he couldn't find the cigarette. So he reached for another one. With it halfway up he saw something bobbing under his nose to the involuntary mumble movement of his mouth. 'Stupid!' framed in his eyes. Then he threw the extra cigarette into the trash can. 'What'd you do that for?" his brain jerked along. His hands shook so badly that the lighter and the cigarette butted. 'Calm down, calm down. It's over for now,' he assured himself. 'But God! This is a nightmare,' he moaned. He did not want anyone coming into his office. The girls in the outer office were busy with typewriters or with calculators. 'Everyone leave me alone,' he wished. 'But it won't end, it just won't ever end,' he whined. Then he shivered, but he was not cold. 'What's he trying to do to me? Everyday, every damn day it's the same. And I can't stand it anymore. Not another time,' his brain squeezed out in pleas. The fluid blurriness before his eyes was not clearing. His heart beat so fast that there was a ringing pressure in his ears. 'Did you tell him you quit? No. Good! Because you can't quit. Oh God! You have to stay and let him yell at you like you're nothing.

Everyday, and I can't again. I just can't stand it anymore!' The cigarette smoke came out in ragged spurts. And these broken exhales sounded like the sobs of a frightened child. So he remembered a fight that he had been bullied into as a small boy. He had cried so rackenly that he couldn't even tell his mother what had happened. 'Mommy!' he now cried . Then he looked up suddenly. Because the girls had stopped their office noises. Had they heard him? Was he talking out loud? He did not know. So he took more deep breaths. But behind his eyes exploded with heat, and the fuzziness of his vision became blinding and these exhales came in ragged spurts also. 'Why did they stop? I don't know. Well think about something else. Anything else. Think about Carol. Think about the kids. Think about being home tonight. You'll be safe there then. But they're why you have to let him yell at you. It's for them. It's because of them. So it's their fault. I could tell him off if it weren't for them. Really tell him off but good. But that's not fair. Fair! What's fair! To hell with fair! Because I just can't stand it anymore. Not another time. Wait! Someone's coming! Oh God, no,' he begged.

"Mr. Hurst, here's the production report for yesterday. We shipped four hundred and eighty dozen slips and two hundred and eleven dozen sleepwear."

He nodded okay to whoever it was without looking up. Then no one was there. And the office noises resumed outside. 'Must have been Billy Joe. Billy. Or Joe. But not Billy Joe. Two first

11

names for a name is stupid. Leave it to southerners to saddle their kids with two first names. We're stupid. I'm stupid. Everyone's stupid. Everything's stupid. Those slips out there are stupid. But mostly I'm stupid though. Yes, that and a coward. Yes, a coward also. Stupid and a coward. Why didn't you tell Mr. Friedman to go to hell if he didn't like the way you run the plant? Because you're a coward. Because of Carol. Yes, because of Carol.' This last he said as though the name had become a heavy weight that he had to drag around. 'She pretends we're somebody important just because I'm plant manager and this is the only plant in town. She struts about putting on airs while I get yelled at everyday. And in front of my people too. Lord, what they must think of me. Everyday and always in front of my people. And I never talk back. Never even answer. I just nod and look scared. He knows I'm a nothing. My people know I'm a nothing and worst of all, I know I'm a nothing,' he moaned again as the not cold shivering came again.

'Okay, okay. Easy boy, calm down Ralph. Get back to work. It's over for now. Maybe it wasn't as bad this time. But you know it was. And always in front of my people. And I never talk back. Never even answer. I just nod and look scared. He knows I'm a nothing. My people know I'm a nothing and worst of all, I know I'm a nothing,' he moaned again as the not cold shivering came again.

'Okay, okay. Easy boy, calm down Ralph. Get back to work. It's over for now. Maybe it wasn't as bad this time. But you know it was. And always in front of my people. And you never talk back, even when you're right. You really are a nothing, Ralph. An absolute nothing.' A new cigarette was lit with still fear shaking hands. 'Where's the other one? There in the ashtray. It's out. Lord, you've got to change jobs. You just can't stand this, not another time. Never again. But you've been sending out resumes for over a year. But no one wants you. Because you're a nothing, a real nobody. But the kids think I'm something. But they're just kids. And they'll learn soon enough. Carol knows you're a nothing though. She's never said so, but she knows. Her with her airs, but deep down she knows. She isn't fooling anyone but herself with her airs. And I'm not fooling anyone but myself. Because everyone knows. They do. Especially about me. Because my eyes say I'm a nothing. Because I smell like a nothing. And fear can be smelled a mile away. Wait! A phone's ringing. Where's the phone ringing? Someone answer that damn phone!'

"Mr. Hurst, Mr. Friedman wants to see you in his office," his secretary said, standing there in the doorway.

'Quit blinking and say something. She's standing there waiting. Say something stupid!' So he nodded, then she was gone.

'Oh God, oh God, I can't, Oh God no, not again, I can't take it again. Not again. It isn't worth it. I just can't. Please leave me alone. Carol! Carol help me! Oh God help me! I can't stand it anymore. What did you do wrong this time? Think! What? Nothing stupid. He doesn't need a reason. He just yells and yells, and you just stand there and take it and take it. Because I'm a nothing. The phone! Oh God, the phone again!'

"Mr. Friedman said he wants you in his office right now."

But 'oh God no!' was all his eyes could see.

BRENDA

I do not have the right to think of you in that way. So I force myself to not think of you in any way. Then suddenly you pass, bright and alive and blond, and I realize that you have been constantly in my thoughts in every way.

MATTIE

She is pale. And she sits very still and with a stoop, and she works. And only her fingers and her hands move, and now and then her arms. And this is the way it has been for so long. Eight hours a day, sometimes nine, and sometimes Saturday mornings, for all of the years that she and Jimmy have been married. She has ushered four pale children, and she works. And her hands are always red and rough, and they are hard calloused in certain places.

She appears as a forever, there in her straight back wicker seated chair in front of her sewing machine. And each of her days repeat themselves in an endless parade of pretty bold colors and bright new fabrics, and the harsh noise of the all around machines and the everywhere rushing. Some of the women fiddle and fidget and gossip though. But Mattie only steadily works here in her closed world. Here in her small world and drudgery of work. She sits even more still today because she hurts. And she cannot find a comfortable position, so she just sits even more still with her hurt. Her left ear continues to ring from Jimmy's quick slap last night. And her breathing is halted, because below her right breast is bruised from her fall against the table. But it was not Jimmy's fault, not really, and she understands this, and she must work so her family can exist.

But Mattie did not like piecework nine years ago, just after she and Jimmy were married, when this plant first came to their town and she became one of the very lucky to be hired. Because the final responsibility for her pay would be entirely hers, rather than the vague responsibility of a time clock. But during a week of training and then a week of experience, piecework gradually became a friendly certainty that Mattie could trust. Because the number she finished multiplied by the rate, became her pay. So these building block numbers became what Mattie thought about most of the day, day after day. Building block numbers, and finding better ways and simpler ways, and therefore faster ways of finishing. Because here there was much that she could control as she worked against the clock. But outside of here there was so little that she could control. So with the last bell every afternoon she would begin to calculate the number finished times the rate for each style, then total all of the styles for that day, and add this to the other days of that week. Yes, there was much that Mattie could control here. So she would lean back from her stoop and smile a small smile and watch as the building blocks built. Only after this routine did she once again begin to think about her own drab clothes, and how tired she always looked, and how whiny the children were, and how ugly the unpainted rented house was. And know the hopelessness of their ever having a nice home of their own.

Mattie never wonders about the thousands and thousands of collars that she has set on the thousands and thousands of womens' suits. Because that is yesterday. She only knows that today some are wide and some are narrow, and some are wide and long and some are narrow and short. Some have sharp points and some are rounded, and some styles pay more per piece than other styles. Mattie is quite skilled, and her collars do not come back because of bad workmanship. Mattie is very fast, and she has the exact feel for the different fabrics and the different styles after only a single trial setting. She does not wonder about the many many women who wear these pretty suits, or about the lives that they have. She does not despise her life. She just assumes that their lives are better.

The silver whir of the long needle does not frighten Mattie now. She has three neatly raised small mounds for scars along her right index finger to show that she has overcome that fear. Each time happened so suddenly, and there was very little pain and only a drop of blood. So she just pulled the broken needle from her finger and applied a band-aid, then she inserted a new needle into the machine and continued. Because she keeps her fingers very close to the blurred needle for fast accuracy. And with quick skill she inches the collar fabrics beneath and around and by the needle. While at the same time she moves the knee treadle out to start the machine and in to stop, and with fast accuracy also. And this is the way it has been for so long.

And today she does not let herself think about Jimmy, or last night. Or about what they have become, or how they had hope things would be for them. Because it really is not his fault, and thinking about this would only make her cry. And she understands completely without knowing the actual words. Because Jimmy did not swing at her, he had swung at his terrible frustration. But only she was there. So now she straightens from her forever stoop and shifts her weight to find a more comfortable position. But bursting lights begin to explode before her eyes, so she halts in mid shift. And with gasping breaths the bursting lights gradually dim. Then she smoothes her drab cotton dress to distract the hurt that is below her breast. But her Forelady is again beside her with another bundle of coats and their collars. Because this endless parade must continue. And Mattie must work so her family can exist.

But it had not always been this way for Mattie and Jimmy. Not ten years ago when she was so cute and so popular and so gay. And he was so big and so sure and so rugged. Back when they would have married one day anyway, but then that next summer they had to get married. Back when their town was only a little less of a crossroads than it is today. And it was thought that this plant's coming would bring prosperity. Back before anyone realized that employing most of its women but only several of its men would cause more problems than it solved. Because working women and unemployed men cannot make the solid families that make a prosperous town. Because then the men have too much time for fighting and for drinking and for messing with the young girls who are waiting to get on at this plant. But for several days a month Jimmy hauls pulpwood logs to the railroad crossing. And in season he helps out on the local farms. And in season he pumps gas for the tourists at the filling station. But mostly Jimmy waits, not knowing for what. Jimmy slapped Mattie, but he did not know why. He knew that he was drunk, but he did not mean to slap Mattie. Not Mattie. But nothing seemed good to him anymore, and everything seemed bad. And he did not think it fair that not one thing had gone as they had hoped. And now Jimmy knew that nothing ever would.

The long needle is silver poised. Then it inches down and down then up, now it is a blurred sharp whirr, then it slows to almost the seeing of it, as it readies to stop. The long needle is silver poised again. And during this, Mattie has been kneading and turning the collars' layered fabrics, whether the collar is of linen or of polyester or of wool. She probes it and she twists it. She folds it and she presses it and she pushes it, with her red rough fingers that are hard calloused in certain places. While her knee at the treadle knows the right split second in which to start or to stop the needle. While her knee knows the exact speed needed, whether it is slow or fast or in between. Just as her fingers know the precise fabric preparations and positions that will result in perfectly even rows of yellow thread stitches or pink thread stitches, or black or blue or white or brown, whichever the color. Because all the colors are pretty and bright, here in this work world of harsh noise and all around machines and everywhere rushing.

But this day does not end. And enduring the constant hurt has exhausted Mattie to the point of nausea. Until the building blocks' building is not important anymore. But still this day does not end. And still she appears as a forever, here stooped in her small world of drudgery. And yet she knows that tonight will be in the same pale house with the same pale Jimmy and the same pale children. And that nothing will change, not tomorrow or next week or next month or next year, not ever. Because Mattie's parade will continue until she dies, and for so very long.

FAR INTO THE NIGHT

When they did speak, it was quietly. Hushed words spoken in the night. While they faced ahead, not toward the other. Asking words. Answering words. Rehearsed words spoken in the dark. "Will you tell your parents goodbye for me?" "Yes." First one, then the other. "Will you tell your parents goodbye for me?" "Yes." Concealing emotion words after careful pauses. As they continued to delay and delay the final end. What else could they do? And in between were the long silences. While they puzzled. While they wondered. While silently they tried to understand this final end, without ever really coming to understand this final end. Because it was not simple, and you would agree. More hushed words spoken very politely. Polite to the point of being brittle. Brittle to the point of breaking. This slow wait until the final end. Their final end. While the moments of their separate pain welled and surged beyond them, then joined with the outside wind that carried their pain from the car and through the all around trees and down the hill to the passing lights on the road below. Still, the they that had been their they was ended. It really was. Only their final end remained. And you would agree. But there had been so much. At least it seemed so. Now there was so little. This you knew so. There had been love. Then that ended. There had been loving. Then that ended. There had been lust. Good lust. Man, woman lust, personal lust. Then that ended also. Still, there had been something. Now there was nothing. Only the delayed, the dreaded final end. So the shroud of bleakness and darkness, the shroud of endings, that comes always with first winter was what remained from the all that had been before. While they remembered some of their times together during the long silences. There had been fun times., And times that almost had been fun. There had been very close times. And times that almost had been very close. There had been times when their future together was everything. And times when only their present together was important. But so much of their time just had not been anything. Almost time. Not quite time. As though in their rush they had forgotten to include a something that was vital. And lacking that vital something caused the almost, the not quite. Had they loved too suddenly, without ever really liking gradually? Possibly. Probably. But it wasn't that simple. It never is. And you would agree.

So they just sat there. What else could they do? Because it was truly ended. It was over, so what more could they do? And you would agree that it was over, and all that they could do. If you said, "it's so sad," that would be right. If you said, "it's a shame," and "what a pity," and, "they were so cute together," all these certainly would be correct. Still, they just sat there, in his car. He on one side, she on the other.

That it was ended, they would agree and you would agree and so would everyone else. And they would sigh and think it a pity, and think it a shame that it couldn't work. And you would agree that it couldn't work, while deep down wishing that it would. Like they wished it would. But they didn't want there to be a difference! Would you have thought that there would be such a difference? Would you have thought that nineteen was one thing and twenty eight another? Could you have foretold the contrast? They never dreamed that nine years could be crucial, and would divide. Well, maybe they had feared, and you would have too. But they wouldn't believe, and you wouldn't have either.

For so long, and far into the night, their silences continued and stood with a roar. They couldn't part and didn't want to forget. They couldn't grieve but could regret. And you would agree that grief would make it final, while regret is rimmed with hope. So hope they did and delayed with a reason. It didn't seem possible but somehow it was. The void was there and couldn't be filled. The difference was there and could be seen. Could nineteen be so carefree, exuberant and gay? And you would agree that it is all that and more. That nineteen is lights and noise, laughter and joy, is plain to see. That it is a time and not an age, that should be enjoyed and not mislaid. They didn't blame nineteen and wouldn't have dared. Could you blame so tender a time? But it was ended. It just wouldn't work.

Though it was cold, they had to stay, sharing these last moments that were so dear. That weren't quite dead but filled with decay. So where is the fault? Who tore it down? That twenty eight was the villain isn't true. They didn't blame twenty eight and you couldn't have either. That twenty eight is maturity and purpose is only fair. That there is a time for goals and work and serious ways is surely in the scheme. So the difference was there and is plain to see, but simple it wasn't and you would agree.

Love is glory and rapture and a dream. Say that and it would be true. Say in another place and that may be true. Another time might also be true. But reality is rude and here and now. So you can't say that love conquers all, though sometimes it does. That they hadn't loved would be wrong. That they hadn't tried couldn't be said. Would you have thought the difference so great?

They could cry but that seldom helps. They could harp and accuse but what does that prove? Would you have said a quick goodbye and ended it there? Wouldn't you delay too and share some more? With it finally ended there would be time for many thoughts, each less likely to sooth. So savor they did, and until it hurt. That there at least had been some days and nights so filled explains the delays. That they had touched and they had been meant everything now. It could last. Why wouldn't it last?

If there were a way, it had been tried. He with his wisdom, she with her enthusiasm. Wouldn't you agree that they had tried? But somewhere with the wind and far into the night, it repeated so clear, "don't let it end, don't ever give up." They stayed. So they delayed. Though still not knowing where to fight. Not knowing what to fight. Not knowing how to fight her time and his age. Should caution be cast? Does reason not matter? Still, the risk is worth it, isn't it? Would you agree that the risk should be taken? But wouldn't that come from the heart? And can the heart be trusted? Because this is not play. Because this is real. So they just sat there. That their wants and their needs were so different loomed larger still. So it was ended. So it was finally ended. Their few polite words lingered only to be swept away by this first winter cold. Because the nine years difference really did matter. They were certain that the nine years mattered. They were positive that the nine years mattered. They sat there so convinced. He on one side, she on the other.

The difference is plain. The difference was youth. But they couldn't blame the gem of youth. And you wouldn't have blamed it either. So there wasn't any blame. And there wasn't a future. It had been tried. It hadn't worked. Only this. But their few moments together would be kept. Kept in a close place that wouldn't forget. That couldn't forget. Nine years did matter. Their final end did come. So love works sometimes, and other times it doesn't. And that's the shame. That's the pity.

THE RAISE

Jeff had been telling himself that he would get the raise. And that all he had to do was to be confident. That he had done the job well, therefore he deserved the raise. And now he believed it.

"Of course, Jeffery, come in. Have a seat," Mr. Margolis smiled warmly and motioned toward a chair, in answer to Jeff's question of whether he had a minute.

Jeff knew better than memorize a speech. He would begin confidently, then continue logically, until the raise became the only fair conclusion.

"Mr. Margolis," Jeff began as he settled into one of the matching soft leather conference chairs that were opposite Mr. Margolis' high backed throne-like executive chair, that so towered there with the large door size dark walnut desk in between. "I would like to discuss a raise."

"Certainly," Mr. Margolis said without surprise.

"Well, Sir. I. Well. Uh, I've been shipping supervisor for almost a year, and, well, I think, uh, well, I was wondering whether you think I've been doing okay." But that did not sound very confident to Jeff.

"Why Jeffery, you are coming along splendidly," Mr. Margolis said frankly and openly and without hesitation. "Just splendidly, my boy . I am very pleased with your progress. Why there have only been several occasions when stores did not receive their orders on time."

"Well, yessir. We have had a couple of late shipments," Jeff admitted as he resettled himself in the soft leather chair. "But we didn't have the dresses to ship. Well, they, well, the plants that is, didn't finish production on schedule."

Mr. Margolis leaned toward the large door size desk, and smiled benevolently, "Jeffery, Jeffery, anyone can make shipments when everything is in stock. Am I right?"

"Well, yessir. But it's impossible to make shipments until the plants produce a complete range of sizes and styles." Jeff countered with some confidence.

"Impossible, Jeffery? Impossible? Don't you agree that a good shipping supervisor always finds a way?"

"Well, yessir, I, uh, but it is difficult when - - -"

"Jeffery, my boy, the garment business is a difficult business. You should have learned that by now. Especially we in high fashion dresses. It is dog eat dog, my boy. And what is impossible for others, must be possible for us. And what is difficult for others, must be routine for us. Am I right? Of course I'm right! But do continue with what you were saying. There is no need in our dwelling on your late shipments.

They had not seemed important at the time. Each one only several days late. And he had notified the stores beforehand. But now they seemed like huge personal failures. So he was glad to change the subject. "Yessir. Well, the payroll records since I took over the shipping department show that the orders shipped efficiency has steadily increased, while the total payroll has steadily decreased. This demonstrates the good job I'm doing, and is justification for a raise," Jeff said with suddenly found confidence.

"You are correct that the profit picture in shipping is greatly improved. Very gratifying, my boy, very gratifying indeed. I knew when I hired you that you would be the right man for the job. Yes, you really are coming along splendidly, Jeffery. Why there have only been a few incidences when overtime reached the danger level. I have a note here somewhere," Mr. Margolis said as he began to look into stacks of papers. "Let's see, where did I put that note? Ah yes, here it is, 'see Jeffery re overtime for weeks ending 3/7, 3/14, 4/1, and 4/8'," Mr. Margolis read. Then he carefully placed the note before Jeff on the dark walnut desk, as though it were new and terribly incriminating evidence. And true sadness came to his eyes. "My boy, overtime can cripple a company. It most certainly can. Why if it got out of hand here, even for only several weeks, we could be out of business. Just that quickly," he said as he snapped his fingers. "Of course these few incidences here of yours are not crippling to us, not in and of themselves at least. But they do indicate that you still have much to learn. And they indicate that you tend to be careless, my boy." This last he said as though announcing a death in the family.

"But Mr. Margolis, those weeks followed our just concluded two big spring promotions. So it was natural that extra order pickers would be called in. And that overtime would briefly increase. So we could fill the additional shipments," Jeff said in excited protest to his death announcement.

"Natural, Jeffery? Natural? Are you positive that every extra order picker was absolutely necessary? Are you positive that every overtime hour was absolutely necessary? Could not iron fisted supervision on your part have gotten the job done with fewer of them?"

"Well, yessir, uh, but it would have been diff---. Uh, yessir, I guess it could have," Jeff finally admitted in bewildered defeat. He had come for a raise. Instead, he was about to be fired. Where had it gone wrong?

"Now Jeffery," Mr. Margolis said as he rose full length from out of his high backed throne. "You want a raise. And you feel that you deserve one. And that is quite understandable. But I want you to see it from my position. So you come around here and sit in my chair, and I will sit where you are. And we will have this conversation again. Remember, you are Mr. Margolis, President. And I am Jeffery, shipping supervisor."

Jeff felt swallowed by the throne. But Mr. Margolis did not tower so, there on the other side of the large door size desk. Still, that did not help very much, and Jeff's palms had begun to sweat badly. He felt silly. And he felt that this conversation had become a comedy, with him the brunt of the joke. Jeff wished that he had not started it. And he so wanted it to end.

"Mr. Margolis," Mr. Margolis said to Jeff, "I would like to discuss a raise."

"Certainly," Jeff said to Mr. Margolis. But the word came out cracked, and it sounded high pitched to Jeff, so he could not keep back a silly smile.

"Sir, I've been shipping supervisor for almost a year now, and." And the conversation continued. And it shifted from one to the other, just as it had before. Because Jeff did not dare deviate from it. And when it again reached the 'iron fisted supervision' place, they concluded it, then again exchanged seats.

"Jeffery, I am not making light of your request," Mr. Margolis said, as would a devoted father to a wayward son. "Your coming to me shows maturity, my boy. And I respect that. And I ask you to trust me. I have never lied to you. I told you when I hired you that if you succeed, I would reward you. And I will. I always keep my word. You are progressing splendidly indeed. But you must be patient, my boy. Young people are so impatient these days . Patience Jeffery, patience is a wonderful trait."

"Yessir, but," Jeff immediately wished that he had not started again. But having started, he could only continue stumbling along. "If as you say I'm progressing splendidly, don't you think that a raise would be an incentive for me to do even better? I think I've been doing a good job, and I enjoy the work. If only you would, if only there were a tangible sign, something definite, to show that I really was doing a good job---."

"Jeffery, my boy, Jeffery, Jeffery, Jeffery," Mr. Margolis said as though he were terribly wounded by all this. "What do you need with money? You are not married, and you do not have any real outside responsibilities., You are not starving, are you? No, of course not. Your clothes are nice enough. And your car still has a lot of good years left. Now I ask, what would a small raise mean to you? Very little, actually. Certainly it would be the easiest thing in the world for me to give you a ten cents an hour raise. But what possible difference would that make?" Mr. Margolis said with almost tears in his eyes. "Four, maybe five dollars more each week. That is not money, Jeffery, not really. Our company is growing quickly, my boy, and you are growing right along with it. Why soon you will be a vital member of our team. Believe me when I say that there are far bigger things in store for you than a mere ten cents an hour raise. You are still young, and you are very bright. Why who knows, one day you may well sit here in my chair. But patience, Jeffery, remember what I said about patience."

"Yessir," Jeff said as he got up to leave. "Thank you for your time." Well at least he had not been fired.

"Anytime, my boy, anytime at all. I am your industrial father, and I am here to help whenever I can. Feel free to come in anytime something is bothering you. That is what I am here for," Mr. Margolis said with glistening eyes, as he and his throne towered so.

WITH MORNING STILL SO FAR

One day she said to me with the abrupt rush of closely held anger, "There has always been a bright morning for serious fiction writers in Wales. Even the learning ones. We cherish them while they are alive. And long after death. Forever even. Here though, morning itself, any kind of morning, is still so far. Here they are never cherished until they are dead. If then. And usually not even then. Yes. Here, with morning still so far, it is bloody well terrible. For you. Yes. For all of you serious ones." Then another interruption and the moment was past, the conversation ended, her close anger ceased with the remaining anger forced back deep inside again.

So it was to her bookstore that I always went during those days to await nervously and to beg if necessary for the calm and the comfort that possibly would be made available to me there at her bookstore whenever comfort became something that became lost from elsewhere all around me, and its having stolen calm snatchingly sneakingly with it too. My escaping quickly and briefly on a run from here and sighing heavily all the while all the way there to her bookstore and being driven to there practically whenever the hard writing of long fiction stumbled for me and staled and became rotted and sour for me, whenever the point and the purpose and the direction and the utter hope of it all for me became faded and jaded and scattered and had drifted into sad disillusions only, whenever my few remaining close friends once again withdrew in silence into their private selves private worlds and quietly raised their cold barriers leaving me outside again stranded again and so harshly alone and so lonely missing them and the true they that I thought they became when with me and the true me that I thought I became when with them, whenever I had absolutely no other safe and warm place anywhere else in which to hide, it was to there to her bookstore that I went sulking low and raw to plead for admission and for a scrap of attention. Because usually she was far too busy behind the counter with customers for more than a mere passing greeting with me. A quick, "Hello, and how is my favorite author, must run, busy you know, " merely this hardly anything and then nothing more. But sometimes, sometimes we would really begin to talk and she would become genuinely interested and eager and involved and I would become filled with surging gratitude as our conversation carried us both along until her bad phone rang loud to end whatever we had begun as I waited and waited and hoped but customers came and went and others came and her bad phone rang again and again and once again her bookstore business had surrounded her and crowded her and smothered her as her large brown eyes became vacant to me and deaf to me and gone to me as I could only stand there wishing and wishing and hoping for her return to me. Other times though she would see my lonely approach, and then she would walk suddenly along the inside long aisle of books and go quickly and close the hard door to her back office behind her to avoid completely any and all contact with me, there being no space or sympathy whatsoever within her on that day at that time except for the pressing and the frantic business business of her bookstore. And these open slams brutal slams locking me out completely did truly wound and hurt as the embarrassed clerk would have to say that she was not in and then both of us would have to wade around uneasily in that cruel lie. But I do not think that it was me particularly or expressly or that it was something mean and intentional on her part because this was, it had to be, her only survival reaction to far far more bookstore obligations and pressures than she could ever deal with cope with, with tolerance and ease until finally her last hiding place became the back office while my last hiding place was her and her bookstore. Because now and then we truly did have splendid conversations that made us both pleased and proud, that we both could savor and save to later remember. So now and once again it was to her bookstore that I went sulking low and lonely for the pot luck of how it would be for me with her today.

To her long shelved high racked books books books I did go trudging again my sulking way tenderly. Groping confused and frantic and without will, but always warmly welcomed usually, except sometimes now and then. Because here I could enjoy myself simply. Here I could enjoy myself without limits, like a toy maker in a toy store, here surrounded by the deep stacked gaudy and commercial books books, her bread basket they, her chaser away of the screaming demon creditors who are ruthless in their endless pursuit. But books books books none the less and therefore grand, a quiet temple on high if you will though in reality it was probably more a loud circus upon a vacant field. Here surrounded by the worst that writers are writing today, because the worst is what the readers demand, these books books with their lusty facades and their phony thicknesses to suck in the suckers and do, to spoon feed them like pouring nothing into nothing. But at least here there is a place where whatever books books may be displayed and are and are bought at least sometimes and are read at least sometimes if rarely their being mostly for show. So this is a partial freedom and a partial availability Though hollow and narrow and cheapened, but free and available to an extent if not completely since a sorry compromise is maybe better than no free and available place whatsoever, though only barely just barely it is. But now and then a fine good book sometimes did slip through unnoticed, overlooked, dismissed, my two books had, so we had fooled them and she knew it. We two knew it, her and I, as did several others too, and still others would learn our secret when they were not looking, when they least expected it, it sneaking up on them and grab seizing them blinded and unaware like they are and they reaching for trash but getting gold instead with the big laughing joke being on them. But don't tell anyone. Listen now, hush. Don't tell anyone. Our secret this, or a shadowy someone will come to maim and to trample the thin few plain books mine among them. Hush, listen now, hush, silence, tiptoe, listen, do not even whisper our secret, be still, so so still, hush. My books had slipped through. Others had, others will, but I won't tell a soul and don't you, promise? Promise now or the shadowy someone will come heavily suddenly. She kept them in a dark alcove way down the wall where he never would think to find them. Isn't that funny? The trick of it, the genius of it, and he has never yet suspected, so don't you tell him. Promise? Have you ever seen the raw mutilations that he performs upon the frail spines of fine books that are to be returned? Can you even imagine the filthy foul deeds that are committed upon them as he readies them for shipment back to the publishers for recycling back into pulp then into paper once again to reappear reincarnated but this time into a proper commercial gaudy book? So avoid the dark alcove. Do not even look in that direction. And do not tell a soul. Promise? Here at her bookstore where I enjoy simply and without limits, the good together with the bad, this tainted temple with its horrors of publishing and publishers.

Her hair of clean strands of grey and of black, and all shiny and tidy in short curls about her neat face prim with her nose small slender and true and her lips pink full and moist, with rosy always in her cheeks, while her years have begun to almost settle in thin short lines about her neck. This so pretty woman from far yonder Wales who speaks our same language correctly without effort, while I speak it rudely almost with careless disregard and am very aware of the contrast in our speech. The heavy desk between our big chairs a pleasant scramble of stacked publishers catalogues and authors announcements and book review clippings. Then she said, "Well you are supposed to suffer," only that, just like that. Directly, openly, and without hesitation. Flinging it even.

But that was not what I had come sulking low to hear. So I let it go on by without deflection. I ignored it, refused to hear it. And I continued uninterrupted with how so very dismal things were with my fiction writing. Its no prospects and lost point and gone future, this while calm and comfort actually were seeping in gradually and

35

reassuringly because hadn't I caught her on a perfect perfect day our best day ever with us talking long already and well as more calm and comfort seeped in from the high walled books books books even there behind me with the secret alcove close by where important chunks of me personally reside standing forlorn upon a dark shelf. Warmed through and through I was by her and her bookstore and our secret, getting lazy even like a hound in a dusty yard in spring. But coldly she said again, and louder this time, "Well you are supposed to suffer," just like that, it flung harder this time, and straighter, not going on by this time. So I heard it and could not ignore it, it piercing me coming from her coldly as an arrow would, whirring and deadly, piercing me deeply and sharply to the very quick. And I stiffened and I pushed myself farther back into the big chair, braced, crouching, threatened now like a fury something cornered. "Why!" an instinctive defensive counter attack thrown out wildly to strike all around at the same time whatever it would. But she only shrugged her hands in her lap, and she looked steadily at me with her eyes brown soft and black lashed gently.

"I am!" Striking out wildly and all around again. "I have, and I am!" But her small smile was sly and knowing and approving even, and teasing and pretty.

"Why, huh, why? And where is it chiseled in stone that writers must suffer?!" The drain and the crush and the terror of the long long years of suffering having ripped wet strips of me from myself, my suddenly remembering it all and fully too, this with her there so damned unconcerned as though I were engaged in a so nice stroll across a park in an afternoon's warm breeze.

"Go ahead and make a dramatic scene of this for a story someday if you must. But we are only having conversation." Said she wiser than me.

But I was not going to take anymore of this. Didn't have to, wasn't going to. Not this sly abuse, this pretty teasing. Me already shot through and wounded, with calm and comfort chased and gone. So I rose quickly and went in hard strides to the door.

"In Wales we love for our writers to be spoiled brats. Rotten buggers through and through. The worse they become, the louder the tantrums, the more they are loved. Then when finally they become liars and cheats and drunks too, they are loved best of all. Being all these is what writers are supposed to be. Just as they are supposed to always suffer.   The longer and the harsher the suffering, the better their writing."

"I have suffered, and I am." Me stopped at the door, looking back with clear anger, my hand hard on the knob. But my words were quiet, the wild fight having begun to leave. Besides, she cared. She did truly care, and today proved it. So I could not leave until forced to, actually.

"And is your writing better?"

"Sometimes."

"See."   Her figure trim, soft breasted and good hipped, delicate there in the big chair, slim hands white folded in her lap.

"But why can't there ever be recognition? Why can't there ever be any appreciation? Why the endless silence? Why can't people become thrilled once again by writers and writing?" Me going slowly back to the big chair. The sharp anger over and quickly leaving. But bitterness about the long suffering returning.

"Why, why, why? You really are spoiled. A spoiled little tyke you are. Isn't that precious? But everyone ignores him. Everyone hates him, no one loves him. Ah, poor little tyke, are you going to eat some worms?" Her pretty smile getting wider and prettier.

A blush pushing itself through the returned bitterness. "Maybe I do exaggerate some. But I live the 'whys', and they are real to me."

"Ah, you would be a favorite in Wales, you really would. I imagine you could be the bloody devil himself once given the proper stage."

"I admit to wanting to be pampered too when the writing is finished for the day." The blush quite bright now.

"And well you would be in Wales, and well you would be. And more, much acclaim I should imagine, especially in our pubs in the evenings. They are our amusement centers, our town meeting halls, our sports places all rolled into one. They are our real entertainment just like the telly is to people here. Unlike your bars here, though, the entire family goes to their favorite pub there. But then Wales is a small country and a very old country, and our pubs are a trusted institution. We are a people who like to gather, and like to share, probably a hold over from our clan days. Everyone is considered family whether related or not. And anyone who is gifted, whether musician or writer or teacher or athlete, is showered with acclaim, and pampered as I said, and encouraged, and freely given a place above the rest. This happens outside of our pubs also. In our magazines, newspapers, on radio and television, around supper tables, while shopping even, everywhere in our daily lives. After all there aren't that many of we Welsh, so there is more than enough national and personal pride to share freely with those few of us who excel. While here, the United States is so immense, both in land and population, and there are many many here who excel. Many many in every type of effort, until they get smothered under the crush of them all. Here, to excel is common, it's expected, in fact to not excel is the surprise, the disappointment, and yes, the disgrace. We are not as intolerant and competitive with each other in Wales. It is enough for us that we still cling to our rocky black mountains, nestle in our blue green valleys, and perch upon our brown golden coasts. And that we gather in the pubs in the evenings to boost our own. I should think that we are rather remarkable for that. On the other hand your people have sprawled across a large region of the world with an industry and a fervor that has never before been know. It is simply amazing. Here you are all crammed in, there you are all scattered out endlessly. Simply amazing, really. But never are you actually one people, and rarely are you ever even close with each other except in cliques and other small groups each with its own identity and direction and goal. Quite boggling it is. And adjusting to this constant busy busy busyness of your people has been rather difficult for me. Often I feel I haven't handled it well at all. But it is just so awesome here for me in a quite exciting way. Rather like a roller coaster ride I should think, and being thrilled and frightened together. But I confess to being homesick for my Wales and our continual rain and damp and fog. The weather here is almost too perfect. Mostly though, I miss feeling secure, miss feeling as though I could ever belong. And I question whether your people feel all that secure, and that they feel as though they belong here."

And again she shrugged her hands in her lap. "But then I'm sure the older ones do. They have already carved out their own private place somewhere here. It's the young ones who are rootless and searching. Sort of like each generation being another generation of pioneers."

Her small smile teasing and pretty again. "You see we don't have that in Wales. Nothing like that. Similar perhaps, but not nearly to that extreme. Everything is almost too exaggerated here. Boggling it is. I should imagine that England is bloody well glad to be rid of you people."

"I should imagine." Said I, smiling wide and proud for my own rowdy people anyway. 'Will you ever return to live in Wales?"

"Oh, of course, of course, yes, certainly, my goodness yes, after all am I not Welsh! And though we may stray far, we don't stray for very long. This has been a working holiday of sorts for me. On the job training I believe you call it here. My mum is looking about now for a shop for me to lease in my town. But it will be a bookshop rather than a bookstore. A cozy place for browsing it will be. Nothing like this. This is boggling it is."

But it would be too forward of me to ask if she would stock my thin books in her shop, too great an assumption upon our new friendship, though suddenly in a rush that was what I wanted more than anything I had wanted, ever. But then I did not know whether

40

the export and import of books was too complicated, more aggravating than the results were worth. So I could only sit in silence.

"You will send me a carton of your books. You will won't you?" Said she, brushing aside the awkward silence that had risen above me. "Of course you will. That would be splendid. And I will display them in the window where they should be, where they belong, not hidden simply because they are not commercial. Then your morning will no longer be so far. And when I tell all my customers that you are a bloody mad and raving writer from the States and my wild spoiled friend then your books will sell well and they will be carefully read and you will have the following that you never will have here. And if you should come to Wales on holiday and be bloody drunk and raging and brawling and perhaps cheat and lie a bit., then you will be championed and toasted in the pubs in the evenings."

And then for those few several brief moments I became famous and read and treasured, and this feeling was grand, indeed it was, there in the pubs of Wales in the evenings surrounded by the loud drinking and the hoarse shouting and the pounding back slapping. Where for once, for the first time finally and totally, my hard labor and clear insight and long learning struggle were appreciated and rewarded. Where I could stomp and brag and prance myself even, because I could do a fine thing with pen and paper that so few others could do, and those surrounding me agreed whole heartedly. But this brief grand feeling could not last and it did not last because then I remembered completely how the

41

many people here had told me scoldingly and quickly to grow up to act my age whenever I began to act only sensitive even, only that, which is a long way before acting temperamental, and much farther still from acting horrible. How whenever I proceeded still on my way to acting temperamental only, they would shrug impatiently and be disgusted and seem put upon and then ignored me for being childish and silly and turned their backs to me rudely and would leave me all alone without an audience, and what is the fun in that?, none and not any for sure, because we serious writers must have a time and a place in which to act spoiled and to be horrible little boys throwing horrible temper tantrums before an audience or else where is the pleasure after writing, where is the satisfaction after writing, where is the release from writing after writing? That vital, vital release of all that is pent up and yet cannot be spent. Because in the endless solitude of hard creation everything becomes warped and exaggerated far beyond what is reality and reason, and the five percent of extra torment that is not written down and cannot be written down must have a suitable escape somehow and somewhere because it will not just evaporate by itself and it does not store well and it can become a real crippler if not allowed to vent itself as boasts and brags and the yelling of pure bullshit. But the people here would not tolerate this from me in any form and would not allow themselves to be near it even and refused to discuss it even, because to them the showing of any emotions other than the blandest of simple emotions they considered this to be a perversion of the foulest kind until love and hate and friendship even were not to be expressed or shown as

42

they are and as they should be with the people there vacant mirrors only. Except her. She cared indeed. She cared enough to understand, and to explain it by saying, "Well writers are supposed to suffer," while she knew that it must escape afterwards somehow and somewhere by venting itself upon an audience. So I sat in the big chair there and for the few brief moments of the grand feeling wished I had been born Welsh, or at least were there in Wales for holiday where serious writers always are approved and applauded. And she sat watching me quietly and smiling slyly and wisely knowing where my thoughts had taken me, and how far, and enjoying those brief moments herself even because obviously I was enjoying them hugely there basking warmly in them so.

Then her bad telephone rang loud, and we both tensed and jerked at the abruptness of the ring that broke our thoughts. Then she was talking with a book salesman. And just that quickly she had been taken from me and our us talking well and long that now had ceased to exist and was gone just that fast. Because she had returned to the cool impersonality of her bookstore business and she would not return to me and our us talking until another day, perhaps, hopefully, but possibly not, ever again even since today until now was the best day ever for the our of us, talking, and it probably never could be improved upon here anyhow and bettered so it should not be tried again even, fighting the constant fight for her time and attention here, but certainly it could happen and it would happen again in Wales. But good times between friends can be only so good and then good only once in that one special way and perfect then only if you both are very lucky and you both work

43

at its happening and if you both leave it alone forever afterwards and never try to recapture it exactly and in that first one particular way because you cannot since then it could only turn out as almost as nearly as only something similar the next time and not quite as good and never again exactly or perfect. So it is best to just walk away from it, leaving it intact, to later remember sweetly. But in that new place in that new time, with each of us a little different and a little better, in far yonder foggy Wales the our of us will talk again long and well and I can wait until then.

So I walked out quickly, leaving it the way it was, and I shedded easily the jilted feeling of her sudden business change, because that complete alteration was all right with me now. And I headed once again back to my long toil going fast now down the long shelved high racked books books books with their tired thickness and their gaudy covers, not daring to notice the dark alcove where I reside in thin volumes between plain coverings, while knowing full well the mutilations that are performed upon publisher returned books.

TOEROW

Before tractors were widespread, farmers called someone who only thought he knew how to plow behind a mule a toerow, because a toerow had to keep his toe in the row to know where the row was.   Commercial clammers now use toerow to describe someone who only thinks he knows how to clam.

The guy that I was bullraking with that day was quite a bit younger than me. His dad and his older brother had been top clammers at different times over the years until it broke them, just as it always breaks even the strongest and the best finally.   Now this guy was top clammer, and he would be until it finally broke him too.   His knowledge of clams and his determination toward clamming were a wonder indeed. He said the secret was simply to picture a dollar sign, then concentrate only on that dollar sign, forgetting about the exhaustion and the monotony and the pain, and pull the bullrake like hell again and again all day long.   But there was much more to it than that, certainly the gift of an instinct for clams, but I had come to it too late in life to ever acquire that much more. Because only those who begin something while very young are given such a gift of instinct, but then not everytime, and not equally, and that is why it is a gift.   Still, I had become fairly good at clamming, through persistence and a lot of trial and error, and my daily totals were close enough to his so that it wasn't too awfully embarrassing for me when we sold to the clam buyer. And for two loners, we got along pretty well. We usually started out each day working different places, but by early afternoon we would have sort of drifted over and would be working the same place. Back then I used to talk quite a bit about being a commercial clammer to anyone who would listen over beer in the evenings at the Jolly Roger. The guy would just sit beside me, leaning on the bar and enjoying his beer, and just look ahead without having very much to say about anything.

On that particular day we were bullraking a thick shell place and were getting fifteen to twenty clams a pull, which wasn't a bad average. But all of a sudden we couldn't buy a clam, well, maybe two or three clams a pull. I looked and the guy had his bullrake in his skiff and was standing there waist deep in the water. I kept pulling like hell though, because while the guy was taking the break was my chance to narrow the gap on him, if only by two or three clams a pull. Then the guy said, "tide's turned, clams're down here, let's find another place." I said, "yeah," after a moment, got up my bullrake and started for my skiff. But I didn't know that the tide had turned. And I didn't know that clams went down when the tide turned. And I didn't know that there would be another place where the clams hadn't yet gone down. That evening at the Jolly Roger I told anyone who would listen that clams went down when the tide turned. The guy just sat beside me and just looked ahead without having very much to say about anything. Yeah, we got along pretty well for two loners.

AND FIND NO DAWN

Surely you've seen her. She stands on the cutbank edge before the deep ditch there beside the paved road. And slowly watches all who pass, from appear to disappear. Or she stands further away, over there in the open field among the plowed rows. And slowly watches all who pass. Sometimes though, she walks her age careful footsteps along the hard rutted dirt road that comes from the never been painted lapboard farmhouse so forlorn there among the stark tall trees, that is even farther away from the paved road. She is on her way to the end of the hard rutted road. Or to the cutbank edge. Or to stand among the plowed rows. To slowly watch all who pass, from appear to disappear. This worn small woman. This tired forever vigil. Of course you've seen her. You just weren't paying attention. But from now on you damn well better pay attention!

Because Miss Moon will get you, if you don't look out. And that is a for real. And me too. And that is a for sure. Because there is nothing but air between her and us, and she can suck away all the air. Because we simply will not be cool. Because we simply will not act like people. We simply will not. So she is going to cause the dew to fall upon us. That last cold dew. Then we will be dead. Dead as a doornail. Dead as a mackerel. She will have turned out our lights. She will just reach into the pocket of her grey frayed overcoat, and get some hell, and fire our silly asses up. Because we keep spreading our shit in the street. And we will not quit. Because we keep hanging out the dirtiest of our laundry. And we will not quit.   Because we do not understand that there is nothing but space between her and us, and she can quickly move away that space. Miss Moon can. Yes hell she can! Yes, it is true that today is just a baby. But babies also wake, and find no dawn. Do you hear me?   Because she can cause that last cold dew to settle upon anyone and everyone, and at anytime.   Now do you hear me? Because then it will be too late for a conference. Then it will be too late for a prayer meeting. Our holecard will be got. She will have snatched it up. And flung it in the trash. So what of man's sicknesses? And can they be cured? But no one is trying. No, not really.   But no one is taking them seriously. No, not really. But can they be controlled? Or at least contained? You sound like a child with a paper head. But I am infected also. Then lame, you suffer too.   Because payback is one terrible dude. Is payback. Because there are the mean people of the world.   And then there is Miss Moon.   And the mean people of the world call Miss Moon every morning to find out which way she is going to travel. So they can go the other way. Because she can do them in a flash. Do us in a heartbeat. Can't we see that in her flat dull eyes? Then there will be no chance to resign. No skying up, no coasting, no swooping, no skating.   Not from the awful wrath of Miss Moon, there won't be. Because she will buy up our wolf tickets, and cash in all that flimsy cardboard. No tiny sweetcheeks is Miss Moon. She can chase us so fast, our shirt tails will never touch ass. Until those tracks will be our last tracks. Now do you see Miss Moon? Now are you paying attention? Because she endlessly wanders the cutbank edge, and the plowed rows, and the hard rutted road. And she watches all

48

who pass, from appear to disappear. So we damn well better start paying attention. Because, yes, today is just a baby. But babies also wake, and find no dawn. Because she can mark us. She can bust our heads. She can pop a cap in us.

If she comes down where we are, we can just forget it. She can tighten up on us until it will be the worst time that there has ever been. Can Miss Moon. And that is a real for sure, man!

The dishwasher stares into emptiness every chance he gets. He feels quite comfortable with emptiness. Because there is a lot of emptiness in the heart of a dishwasher. And there is a lot of emptiness in the soul of a dishwasher. Maybe that is because no one ever dreams of saying, "my compliments to the dishwasher." What he does is expected, never respected. Say, "fool," to the dishwasher, but you will only get an empty stare without a response. Hell, he knew that long before it occurred to you to even suspect it. Say, "I'll kill you," and believe it absolutely, but still only the stare without a response. After all, there isn't anything that you can do to the dishwasher that he hasn't already done to himself. Dishwashers are very good at self-destruction. You can harm the dishwasher. But you can't really hurt the dishwasher. Hell, hurt is all the dishwasher has ever know. That, and emptiness. The hurt in the dishwasher's life, and the hurt in the dishwasher's soul, and the hurt of the dishwasher's hands, are extraordinary hurts indeed. There simply is not a hurt that is more severe than the hurt of a dishwasher's hands. And the hurt is immediate, beginning when the dishwasher first begins. Then his hands become too white and too puckered from the constant immersion in hot water. Afterwards his hands become too red and too chapped from the constant immersion in strong detergent. When the dishwasher's hands do dry, the skin on them draws and tightens horribly, especially at the cuticles where the skin just lets go from the strain and bloodily pulls back from the nails. And the knuckles and the joints of his hands suddenly have acquired a particularly stressed expression. The acid in the grease and in the food and in the detergent have by now burned away all of the hair on the backs of his hands and the backs of his fingers. The skin on both hands of the dishwasher tingle hurts continually in dry air as though the nerve ends in the skin have been exposed and are raw. Immersion into very hot or very cold water now, and the continual tingle becomes a hurt that is far beyond a hurt alone. An ugly open draining rash has come to the backs of his hands and to the backs of his fingers. The skin on the palms of both hands has become shiny and brittle looking, and the fingerprints have become dim and glossy. The fingernails themselves have become so wear filed that a razor edge sharpness has been honed to them. An unreal and a scary transparency has come to the skin beneath the open draining rashes. The veins and the arteries of both hands have become unnaturally raised, and the blood they contain is a vital blue that somehow soon darkens to a mortal purple. And all cuts no longer heal normally. With the hanging meat pulled away, an eerie whiteness comes to the valley of any cut as though it had been seared with a hot poker. The cut does not bleed. Exposing it to air is maddening. The skin does not come together to heal this cut. Rather, the skin pulls apart and gaps open the cut until gradually the valley flattens and slowly the cut edges round. A loose festered scab comes to the cut overnight, only to be knocked off and floated away at the start of the next day's dishwashing. But the cut does heal, finally, but in spite of everything and not because of anything. And odd protrusions come under the fingernails, as these fingerends have unexplainable indention's somehow pushed into them. Drumming such fingerends upon any surface, hard or soft, produces a steady pounding torture. But if the drumming is kept moderate, the pain of this torture is enjoyable and is soothing even. The knuckles and the joints of both hands are now glassy marbled globes. The skins is now durably cured parchment. These are now the plastic tough hands of a true dishwasher. So the dishwasher can be harmed. But he cannot be further hurt. He already knows hurt very well. Hell, hurt is an embrace that he lives with always. And the emptiness that is in the dishwasher's soul is an extraordinary emptiness. And from the long rutted dirt road, Miss Moon watches this, her tangled grey hair dull and unmoving. And god damn does it turn her crank! She is getting pissed, man! Thoroughly pissed. You better look out!

When the owner growled in harsh admonishment at the always drunk fat cook, "you've been drinking again!", the cook's clouded red eyes replied in puffy mild surprise, "what's the problem? I drink everyday." So the owner just stood there looking and sputtering in complete frustration for a moment. Then he shrugged the hopelessness of it all, and went back out the swinging down now swinging doors, back to idly standing and waiting for all that money to be brought to him there beside the cash register.

After all, a drunk is a drunk, is a drunk, is a drunk, and a drunk is all a drunk will ever be, so what can you do? So the fat cook, his undersized stubby legs hardly able to support the cantilevered weight of his overhanging belly, continued to come his drag ass and taking forever way in from his hit upon again out back beside the fence hidden bottle. He shuffles, rather than walks, with the load, and his meaty big hands paw grab for anything solid that will allow him to pull then to push his way along. Smelly sweat drops in shiny wads from the cook's rolled fat chin and falls splat right into your being prepared food, while the cook wobbly stands his never ending endless hours in front of the blurry hot stove. Ah, the secret seasoning! The special ingredient,. An old family recipe, to be sure. But don't ask for this carefully guarded recipe, you really don't want it. Just eat, eat and enjoy. But for sixteen hours a day, six days a week, at near minimum wage, with terrible conditions, a body only is what is wanted, so a body only is what is got. After all, you get what you pay for, don't you? But it does not have anything to do with suppression or repression, with race, creed or color, with rich or poor, with the haves and the have nots. It does not have a god damn thing to do with anything, anything except business. Simple business. Profitable business. That, and not anything else. The bottom line, that alone. Nothing sinister. Maybe immoral, but not illegal. The dishwasher understands this. Because the dishwasher understands everything. The dishwasher knows this. Because the dishwasher knows everything. That is why the dishwasher strikes fear in the hearts of the others. Because he knows. Because the dirty rotten son of a bitch knows! He knows everything, man! And he has absolutely nothing to lose by using what he knows. Ah! there is the crux of it. Knowing is one thing. But having nothing to lose by using, that strikes fear. Strikes terror, even. After all, the dishwasher already is as low as a man can get. He is at the bottom, and does not want to go up, would not accept up if you gave it to him on a silver platter. What would the dishwasher do with up? Up is for the phonies, for the theys of this world. Dishwashing is for the purists, for the real, for the righteous. Dishwashers do not pretend. And without pretense, they are quick to see the pretense in others.   And seeing these pretenses, knowing them, why not announce them? That is what the righteous do. They announce! From orange crates, from courthouse steps, from anywhere. Announce, loud and long. Why the hell not? After all, what does the dishwasher care? Yeah, he can be a brutal son of a bitch all right. You can take that to the bank, they will cash it. So the others walk on eggshells when around the dishwasher. They tiptoe. Because, from their pretenses, the dishwasher has discovered their worst secret, the one they dread most being known, this without ever having actually seen it or being told it. It just sort of comes to him along with the hurt, along with the emptiness, and suddenly he knows it to be the truth. Then the dishwasher has the others right where he wants them, right where they never and not ever wanted to be. He has them pegged. And they know he has them pegged. And he knows he has them pegged. And they know he knows he has them pegged. And he knows they know he knows he has them pegged. A regular cat and mouse playing game. But it is dead serious. It ain't playing, man, and it sure as hell ain't no game. So the others continue to tiptoe when around the dishwasher . But just like the moth and the flame, they simply cannot stand the suspense. They know that he knows, but they refuse to believe!, that he really does know. Refuse to believe that he really will announce it. So they swear at the dishwasher. Or tease the dishwasher. Or they insult the dishwasher. Or ignore the dishwasher. Anything, or nothing. Maybe the dishwasher just is bored. Maybe he just is in a what the hell mood. Then, abruptly, loudly, their worst dreaded to be known secret is announced as plop a double handful of their shit is spread in the street. "Hey Phil, Ann sucks Vinnie's dick for twenty dollars every morning out back before we get to work!" Jesus H. Christ, he said it! He really said it! And loud as hell too! Patsy suddenly looks as though she had been slapped in the face, standing over there beside the wine cooler chatting with two of the other waitresses. Vinnie looks up startled from making change at the cash register. The customers there look toward the doors that swing. Jesus H. Christ, he really said it. Out went the invitation to the whole damn world to, hey everybody!, come take a good look at Patsy's shit spread out there in the street. Is that a brutal son of a bitch, or is that a brutal son of a bitch? That is a brutal son of a bitch all right. That is a dishwasher for you. But what does he care? Who is he trying to impress? What does he have to lose? So the moral is, fear most those who have the least to lose. Because they refuse to pretend. But look, Miss Moon is standing there on the cutbank edge, her flat eyes grey hot. It is building, man, she is building, building and building, and soon it will happen.

This while small people, evil people, continue to scurry by unaware on the paved road, too preoccupied to notice, too selfish to care. But soon, yes, very soon indeed.

But even the devil himself fears someone. Even the mean people of this world call Miss Moon every day to see which way she is traveling. And it is the silent young cook that the dishwasher fears. The silent young cook appears to be very strong, and the silent young cook is very strong. He can one hand lift and pour a fifty pound sack of flour while making the dough for the fresh baked bread. That is very strong all right. His shoulders are wide, and his arms are big, and his neck is thick. And it is only seldom that he talks. People who seldom talk are either very wise, or they are very stupid, or else they are to be feared. But it is the unexploded presence about the silent young cook that causes the dishwasher to fear him. This unexploded presence completely fills a doorway a second before the silent young cook does. The dishwasher's weapons are his brutal words. But words hurt only if you let words hurt. Words themselves cannot hurt. Even brutal words cannot hurt. But when the silent young cook does explode, the devastation will be widespread. The hurt will be uncontrollable. The dishwasher knows this, and the dishwasher respects this. The dishwasher is a fool, but the dishwasher is not an idiot. Because things definitely will be smashed, things definitely will be trampled, things definitely will be crippled, when the silent young cook does explode. So do not, repeat, do not, screw with the silent young cook. That is a for sure no no. And do not screw with the fat drunk cook either. Because the silent young cook is the self appointed protector of the fat drunk cook. He is his shield against abuse and punishment for not being able to adequately to do his job. What the stupors prevent the fat drunk cook from doing, the silent young cook quickly steps in and does swiftly and surely. But questions arise and costs are incurred, when one is his brother's keeper to another, at the expense of everything else. Who will answer these questions? Who will pay these costs? Is the fat drunk cook truly served by being encouraged to continue his fast downward spiral undisturbed? Is the silent young cook truly the martyred better for living through another? Or, as almost daily the silent young cook becomes even more sullen and remote, is man himself the increasing and the final loser because of this undeserved denial of self, because of this undeserved bolster of another? Hard questions to be answered. High costs to be paid. This while the gradual cancer of his own creation has so eaten away at the silent young cook, until the devastation bomb that is within is now prominently exposed and new metal raw and clearly ticking. Therefore, no smoking, fragile do not jar. Therefore , use no hooks. Do not fold, spindle or mutilate. Because this fucker is about to blow! While under the grey evening sky, among the plowed rows, Miss Moon watches. There she is. Miss Moon is watching all who pass, from appear to disappear.

What is the definition of whore? And how is it to be reconciled? Whore, a prostitute. Prostitute, a woman who engages in sexual intercourse for money. Reconcile, to make compatible. But is it compatible for the restaurant owner to recklessly fire a bus boy for breaking a dollar plate, then just as recklessly, offer a waitress twenty dollars for a quickie? Because there are some few men who cull no woman, regardless of her degree of coarseness or cleanness or ugliness. These men must be with any woman, just as the pack must trapse after any bitch that is in heat. This is a sickness. This is a foulness. And this sickness is in the eyes of these men. And this foulness is in the smell of these men. Because there are no limits that these men will not go beyond. No threat is too great. No lie is too horrible. No blackmail is too dastardly. This while having no regrets, while having no qualms, just having five dirty minutes in any shadow, with any woman. That, and only that. Or even the open fondling of privates in front of other employees, it matters not to these same few men. It is only a matter of whatever they can get away with. They will eventually boast about it to the others anyway. In sight, out of sight, what difference does it make? And it is surprising how many women there are who tolerate and even encourage such men. And even more shocking, consider such attentions as exciting compliments. Though these women are no more to these men than warm receptacles, wet depositories. Hairy legs hoisted skyward before the fly can be unzipped. Drooling lips parted round before the money can be passed. And what will the woman purchase with the twenty dollars, that she cannot let her husband or her brother or her boyfriend or her father know about? What does she see, when next she is with the knowing other employees? Can she keep from looking away, when next with husband or brother or boyfriend or father? And if there is a child, will the child know when next it comes crying and clinging in the night to its mother's teeth bruised breasts, the shame that has gone on there? When the incident has become long ago, and the others have gone their own way, how will the sick man and the whore woman remember it? Will they even remember it at all?

So just keep on keeping on. Go ahead and bite off as much of Miss Moon's ass as you want. But you better make double damn sure that you do not bite off more ass than you can chew. Just make it light on yourself. Remember that what goes around comes around. Because Miss Moon is the last person in the world that you want to get into a pissing contest with. Miss Moon can bust your cap. She can hurt your feelings. Miss Moon can bark here and bite way over yonder. So beware. Pay attention. Forewarned, and all that. Because Miss Moon will get you, if you don't look out. Don't you see her standing there, ancient, grey, timeless and forever? So tiptoe. Yes, for sure tiptoe. Because Miss Moon can knock you down. And babies can also wake, and find no dawn.

YANKEE TOM

You really don't want to crowd a commercial clammer too closely about anything. We're the easiest men in the world to get along with, but the last men in the world that you want to get pissed. Like the time Yankee Tom found a pretty thick spot of clams in a shelly area and made a little over a hundred dollars for the day, which ain't bad. And he figured that he could do about that good the next day, so that was where he was working. Well, he could see Six Pack off in the distance, prowling for clams and not finding any. Six Pack was upriver, then Six Pack was down river, then Six Pack was across river. Yeah, Six Pack was sure enough on the prowl, and Six Pack would crowd you if you didn't watch out. Weekend clammers are all nerve, and their real bad about crowding too. Especially when they see one of us who clams full time, because they know we ain't there ass deep in sea water just farting around for pocket change. But they don't know how to find the spot, and they don't know how to work a spot, and its easy enough to lead them off of a spot, like a hen quail decoys off a predator then circles back around to the nest. But another commercial clammer knows better, and all he has to do is get near a spot, and it won't take him long to find a spot, then he'll be right to work on the spot in a heartbeat. So Six Pack no sooner saw Yankee Tom, then here he was grinning, his skiff throwing a three foot wake in his rush. Yankee Tom never did do much more than grunt now and then for the rest of the day, but Six Pack kept talking buddy buddy and long lost friend until it made you sick. Well, Yankee Tom didn't make close to a hundred dollars for the day thanks to Six Pack, and he was pissed for fare thee well, but still he never said nothing. Then Yankee Tom was sitting on a bar stool hunched over a beer at the Jolly Roger late that afternoon. Commercial clammers always have a big thirst, but we're especially thirsty late in the afternoon after an all day out there of it. So the bar was loudly lined with us on each side of Yankee Tom, he just sat there all quiet and thoughtful like, when in came Six Pack broad smiling and real happy about his a little over a hundred dollar day. Well, in his rush to order a tall cold draught, he pushed in between me and Yankee Tom, bumping Yankee Tom until some beer spilled. Well sir, Yankee Tom just stepped back off his stool and said, "You rotten son of a bitch, you crowded me off of my clams and I never said nothing. But I'll be goddamned if I am going to let you crowd me off my bar stool." And with that, he put a fast hard fist dead between Six Packs eyes and fell that sucker like a stiff tree. Well, that was the last time that Six Pack ever crowded Yankee Tom about anything. But the rest of us still had to watch for Six Pack whenever he was prowling for clams and not finding many.

WHEN FALL COMES COLD

She worked as a clerk in the water department for the city for forty years, each year that followed the last and followed the next and the next and the next and again. And when she retired at seventy years old her monthly retirement checks were larger than her monthly work checks had been. But that was her affair, another of those, and therefore to be secreted, for her to keep to herself just as she kept most of the affairs of her life to herself until seemingly she had no life of her own, until she little more than mirrored the lives of those around her, living more in their reflections, while having so little that was characteristically hers individually hers separately hers, until it was almost unheard of for her to show a deep emotion or state a strong belief or reveal a tender flaw or speak wishfully of the past or hopefully of the future. She was always about, but never of. She was always there, but never here.

But my mother told me that once long ago she had worked at Virginia Beach for several years when she was in her middle twenties when my mother was still in high school. But that she had, only that, was all that my mother knew of those years of her sisters'. Only that fact, nothing about where she had worked, for whom, what had been in her day, who were her friends, where had she lived, was it beachfront and sandy or beyond yet still within the seabreeze, had being there been to go to something or to run from something, why had she returned finally to her hometown, was that something sudden or something planned, had there been a quick and romantic tragic love, had there been no love and no friends and only emptiness and cold tears there at such a wonderful place where emptiness and nights alone and lonely should never be allowed and should be forbidden by law? Questions, wonderings, musings, ponderings, never to be answered. Because that time, too, was her affair. That she had gone, that she had stayed for a time, that she had then returned. Only these facts were ever to be known. That she never married was known and obvious. And the children that she would come to know and to love were the children of her sisters, with her always and only the visiting or visited aunt. And if this pained or troubled or bereaved her terribly, she was never to say or to even hint at because this too and again was her affair. Her affair, again, as were her feelings, whether many or none, on how it felt inside deep for her as a woman to go entirely through her long life without a husband, a lover, a man friend, or even so much as a single date that was ever to be known about.

Because when she returned to her hometown, she returned also to living and working in the boarding house that her mother managed. And when she wasn't busy at the water department, she was busy with the demands of the boarding house. Then her father lost his right arm above the elbow while working in the railroad switching yard. So the railroad made him night watchman at one of the main crossings. But mostly he drank, and finally the railroad retired him. Then her mother became too worn out and ill, and they could no longer manage the boarding house. So the family went to live in an ancient upstairs corner apartment in a coal dusty block of

62

ancient apartments there beside the railroad tracks. But with the clank and rattle of the trains nearby, their whistles low and moaning in passing in the dusk of evening, her father could not remain settled or sane or content or sober, so he went to visit with one of her sisters who was living then for a time beside the ocean at a far distance where it was always warm. There he fished each day from a rickety pier, and he enjoyed being lazy and warm, and mostly he was happy there away from the train sounds that so haunted him. And slowly he died there. Her mother never recovered from being too worn out, and she continued ill and bedridden even and shrillingly complaining for all of the years after losing management of the boarding house. Then her mother died slowly also. But through these many years she remained busy with her water department work, while her sisters remained busy with the raising and the caring of their families. And the difference in their lives and her life became even more clear and stark and set in its contrast, but if she ever longed for a close dream that had been lost somehow or stolen while she wasn't looking by the work and by the years and by the responsibility, it was never known because that again was her affair.

She never owned a car, and she never learned to drive a car. And in the late years after her retirement she became quite demanding of those who owned a car, never fully understanding the expense of a car or the aggravation of going and going here and there constantly continually, shopping from store to store to store without ever buying anything of consequence, and going just for the sake of going and sightseeing relentlessly when only she had the time and the money for such aimless wandering. And often she used her family position to take advantage of a car and its driver, saying, "well, it would only take a minute, but its all right if you don't want to go, it isn't important." Then the old lady pouting and the silence with puffing sniffles, until the other out of guilt, went. And in so going the other became resentful and felt put upon and forced without choice. And in so feeling, the other came to feel even more quilt because hadn't she given of herself to others unselfishly for most all her years, and what was this small expense and brief time that was so very welcome and entertaining to her?

Then in the still later years embarrassment was added to the other mixed feelings of guilt and obligation and wanting to please and being kind. Because with her hard of hearing now and refusing to wear a hearing aid, with her often teetering and tottering now and becoming confused about her intended direction and purpose, but continuing unswayed and iron determined never the less like an unguided yet homed in projectile that is fragile yet hell bent, busting through shopping groups and oblivious of them and of her disruption of them, there going up and down aisles with her long flapping coat scattering stacked shelf items to crash upon the floor sprawling in a wreckage trail behind her passage until at last after having traveled many aisles she would end up at a check out counter with but a single inexpensive trinket item of no consequence, and blindly surge passed the waiting customer line by forging her way unseeing, unhearing, unknowing, totally oblivious to all about but herself there at the front of the line and now in demand of immediate service while being blissfully unaware of the destruction and the disturbance there washing and swirling and ebbing in her wide wake with us cringing and restoring and apologizing. But these were the worst things she ever did, her only short comings, and when compared with what she might have been or might have done were mild and inconveniences only. Tolerances given freely to the old. Because she was never known to lie or to indulge in gossip or to cheat or to bicker or to have a true enemy or to cause intrigues or to cause a personal hurt to another. And to never have done any of these is to have accomplished a great deal with ones' life.

She lived through her long years with patience, with a great calm, as one by one all of her close family died. Through her next to the youngest sister who committed suicide with a straight razor in one of the bathrooms of the boarding house. Through her fathers' finally coming home dead on a train in a box. Through her mothers' last sighing and gagging and dying in the bed in the ancient apartment in the dark of the night. Through her sisters' slow and painful dying of cancer. Then two years later only to suffer through the same thing again as another sister died slowly from cancer too. Then, as though enough was not enough, through the car wreck that killed her last sister suddenly and horribly. But on and on she lived now without close family with her patience and with her calm as it became her nieces' and her nephews' turn with the dice. And within only several years two of them died from heart attacks and one of them died from alcoholism. While the aches and the pains and the grips of middle age began to slow the rest and to cripple some of them. Her tears remained her affair throughout, though, and they were rarely seen by us and then as small and drying tears. She never became overly philosophical or religiously pompous by so much dying and suffering and death, never demanding or accusing or cursing or shouting, "Why!" Rather, saying softly only, "yes, what a shame. So many have gone on. How very much they are missed. Now I am nearly alone here."

Her sister who had been killed was my mother, and for a time after the car wreck she tried very hard to be another mother to me. But I was well into manhood by then and neither needed or wanted another mother, and I handled this with her gently though firmly but without ever speaking of it openly. Because even if I had needed or wanted another mother, she clearly had never been one, and she didn't understand the whole job fully, and her heart wasn't in it not really, and she didn't know all the subtleties that comprise a mother. But for a time, she went through the motions anyway and she tried hard with her awkward attempts being obvious and somewhat inconsiderate, with both of us very uncomfortable with her playing at so different a role. Then we were both relieved when finally she stopped, and she went back to simply being my aunt and my friend.

Not having married myself and not living at a far distance from her, while my two sisters were married with very active families and did live at a fairly far distance from her. So it was expected that I should be the one to visit her frequently. But by then my everyday life had become quite full and demanding and difficult to leave if only for a day, and that was the excuse I had begun to use more and more often to visit her less and less often.

But also she had become very old and withdrawn by then and she seldom went out to shop even, with the teetering and tottering having become stumbling and falling, with her still hard of hearing and usually confused and therefore hard to talk with in a normal way. These, while the ancient apartment continued to be too filled with the drifting and the surrounding and the smothering memories of all the death and the dying and the dead until I could never relax there or enjoy myself there what with the old air there close and stifling and too real with the dark and gone past. So I had not visited her in a long while. Then last week one of my sisters phoned to say that she had been on a long trip with a girl friend to a church conference and while returning they had stopped by for an overnight visit with her. That sadly she was even more infirm and unsound now, was failing badly now and quickly becoming senile, and that her condition could only worsen. That the three of us should begin to think about a nursing home for her.

We sat very still on the ancient couch in the high ceilinged ancient apartment and we looked in silence out beyond the tall windows at what a thin and dreary rain was doing now when fall comes cold to the shivering crisp leaves of the great hickory trees that lined her street like walls. She breathed in through her slightly parted lips, slowly and carefully, and the careful passage of the air could be head in the silence as a slow soft whizzing. She exhaled with her lips now closed, through her frail nose, slow and carefully again, and along with the exhale she hummed quietly to herself for the length of the slow and careful exhale as though the humming was a sure comfort and a reassurance to her with the vibrating hum sounds soothing there inside her nodding head. But these brittle sounds of the very old only added to my uneasiness, and a swelling restlessness came to me, with my own breathing becoming sharper and quicker, with my wanting very much to be elsewhere than here and not under the dark and the gone past again.

"That girl was here." She spoke gently into what had been our long silence, her shriveled face blank and broken, her dull eyes never again to sparkle.

"What girl?" Puzzled, wondering, looking at her.

"You know, that girl." She looked from beyond the tall windows to me there beside her.

But I didn't know, couldn't imagine.

"You know, that girl, what's her name? The one from Florida." Faint testiness had come to her frail voice.

Then suddenly I knew that she meant my sister, Patsy, the one that had visited her last week, the one who had called me, the sister that she had always been the closest to.

"Who? Patsy? Do you mean Patsy?" And a chill of shock and disbelief rose from across my shoulders and it went up my back neck, raising the hairs there.

"Patsy. Yes. That is what the other girl called her. Is Patsy family?" Many brown age spots covered the back of her hands there folded neatly in her tiny lap, her fingers puckered and drawn and pale.

I tried to appear casual. But it was a long moment before I could speak. "She is my sister, and your niece." But a quiver was in my voice.

"I thought she was family. She talked like she was family." Her lips frail and blue and brittle.

Again we looked out into the dreariness that was beyond the tall windows. And in that hard silence I knew how very far she had failed, and that she could never return now except briefly and in glimpses. Because final old age had indeed come to take her. But that was still her affair alone. And that was okay. Because she was going to go away with it with her patience and with her calm as always.

"Who is Glynn? Is he family?" Her hums when she wasn't speaking continued to rest and to reassure her. But they no longer troubled me. Why should they? It was here. It was done.

"Glynn is Patsy' husband." I said as matter of factly as I could, almost making it. Glynn had long been her favorite preacher. And for years whenever she could she was at his church to hear his sermons.

"She mentioned him a lot. I couldn't remember, but I didn't want to ask." Innocently, openly, as would a child.

So new death had come to be with the old dead in this ancient apartment. There has always and only been death and dying and the dead here. And it was here again and done and wouldn't leave now. But better here than to spoil a pretty place. Soon death would have to go find another place. Because my mothers' side of the family would soon consist only of distant and scattered cousins all having gone their separate ways, her family having all gone on, her family having ceased. We would not need this death place again. It has long been coming to this slowly, and is the proper way of things, and cannot be altered anyway, so I said, "okay," to myself in accepting it fully. Then a patience came softly to me, and with it a calmness too, so I sighed resigned.

But when I looked at her, her eyes were wide now and they had cut to look sharply at me with suspicion and fear. Her humming had stopped. Her crippled hands were curled into fist balls in her tensed lap. I smiled. But her sharp look remained the same. Then I knew that she had completely forgotten who I was. That the stranger me there beside her frightened her, who is he, what does he want, where did he come from, when will he leave?

"Why don't you tell me about when you were young and lived at Virginia Beach?"

I could see her begin to come back, if for only a brief glimpse, as some recognition returned to her blank eyes as they narrowed and became dull again.

"Oh my. Oh, that was so long ago. I did though. But that is all I remember. That I did."

And perhaps she didn't remember, not that far back, not back to that long long ago for her. Perhaps that was it. Or probably it was that it had always been her affair, and it would remain so until her end. Probably that was it. But I still very much wanted for there to have been a quick and a romantic tragic love for her there beside the sea back then, that anyway to glimpse upon shyly in her remaining nice moments. Because there had been little other than rude barren life for her since. So I wished this at least for her, now when her fall had come so cold.

THE OLD SEA CAPTAINS

They come every morning to sit on the bench down at Casper's, weather permitting and still alive permitting. The old sea captains, the authorities, the have a sea story to tell about anything, the have an opinion on everything. To kill time between nothing to do and nowhere to go, at Casper's Marina on the bench every morning. Weather permitting and still alive permitting. The old sea captains. To watch the deep water. To watch the wind and the clouds and the tide. To watch the fine yachts passing on the Inland Waterway. To watch us young fishermen docking for fuel at the beginning or at the middle or at the end of our catching day. And to remember. Mostly to remember. And what they cannot remember, they invent. The old sea captains, very busy at this idle work on the bench every morning. Whittling red cedar logs into perfumed toothpicks. Spitting brown tobacco gravy on slick stained asphalt. Sitting hunched against canes. Tying proper sea knots in scrap line. Yarning about when our Holligan Navy whipped the Sunshine Boys in the Pacific, back then. Ah, that was a time. The best time there ever was. The old sea captains. Killing time between nothing to do and nowhere to go. Remembering the slanted squalls, the crashing storms, the engine breakdowns, the boat running agrounds, the close calls, all those who have gone on before. Remembering the good seasons. Remembering the bad seasons. Exactly like today's seasons, except their seasons were forty-five years ago. Still, the more things change, the more things stay the same. But we don't go at the right time, and we don't come in at the right time. We don't boat handle right. We don't gear deploy right. We don't think right.

We just don't fish right. We just don't do anything right. Because they were fishermen, and we are not fishermen. Because they were true salty, and we are candy asses. Because their boats were sturdy, and our boats are wormy. Because they were tough men steady going, and we regularly whine and lean on the oars. Because they knew, we don't. Because they did, we won't. The old sea captains. The authorities, the tormenters, the good friends. The have a sea story to tell about anything. The have an opinion on everything. Whittling, tying, spitting, tormenting, yarning, there hunched against canes. Watching. Inventing. Remembering. Sitting on the bench down at Casper's every morning. The old sea captains. Weather permitting and still alive permitting.

To Oscar Schneider

THROUGH ALL THE LONELY NIGHTS

Through all the lonely nights
with all the changing places,
    through all the solitary days
    with all the passing faces.

It simply never occurred to me
that you finally would not come my way,
    and know right then
    that here close beside is where you would stay.

Through all the harsh sacrifices
with all the bold schemes,
    through all the painful failings
    with all the grand dreams.

It simply never occurred to me
that we finally would not be together,
    and be as one
    through the warm and cold of the whatever.

Whether you were fair or dark
was not my important thing,
    as long as you were pleasant and sincere
    and calmness bring.

Whether I were poor or famous
would not be your deciding thing,
		as long as I were loving and sharing,
		and comfort bring.

But this has not happened
and seemingly now it never will,
		because this cannot happen
		and the why is only a silent still.

Certainly I have prepared
certainly I have sought,
		certainly I have matured
		certainly I have fought.

Certainly you have whirled
certainly you have learned,
		certainly you have waited
		certainly you have yearned.

Through all the lonely nights
with all the changing places,
		through all the solitary days
		with all the passing faces.

Where is it written
that it isn't for us to know,
    where is it carved
    that it isn't for us to sow?

Why must it be
that we can never reap,
    why must it be
    that we can never keep?

It simply never occurred to me
that we would not even meet,
    though surely you are wandering somewhere
    sad on a frantic street.

Forever apart
isn't how it really should be,
    when forever together
    is how it really could be.

It simply never occurred to me
that you would not be here at the end,
    and helplessly there is not anywhere
    that for you I can send.

So a tender so long from afar, only this,

because I have always cherished you as fine,

so a sweet goodbye from afar, only this,

because I have always caressed you as mine.

THE LEGEND

  He had already been a legend for ten years, probably closer to fifteen years, when I moved to Swansboro and began to become a commercial clammer. I had never heard of him before this move, even though I had lived only twenty miles away. But then a legend can be quite local. And a legend can be a specialist whose profound impact does not affect other neighboring specialists. And it is certainly okay if this legend is still very much alive, rather than an often written about fictional character, or an immortalized dead man. Because today the extent to which a man can become has no limits, other than those that he imposed upon himself, because the opportunities really are that plentiful. Sometimes a man becomes exactly what he intends, but this is unusual, and more often than not a man becomes exactly what he does not intend. He may intend becoming just well known, and end up becoming famous. He may intend becoming just notorious, and end up becoming an outlaw. He may intend becoming just selfless, and end up becoming a saint. He many intend becoming just powerful, and end up becoming feared. Or he may intend become just very good at his work, like he did, and end up becoming a legend because of how truly good he did become at his work, like he did. But no man can really intend to become a legend. Because that is just too far beyond the imagination of a man's ambition. And too, time and place and circumstance and luck all have a great deal to do with the creation of a legend. Still, I had never before met an honest to goodness, a real, a large as life, legend. And probably will never another one. And really don't want to. Because one genuine legend in one's lifetime, like one true love, is quite enough.

When I moved to Swansboro everyone had their favorite story about the various feats of Pete the Clammer, and wherever I went along the waterfront during those first years these stories were regularly being told and retold. Often though, they simply said, "remember when Pete the Clammer. . . ," then they just trailed off to nothing, and the others present would immediately fall silent, and begin to nod in awed agreement. Because the favorite stories had become so well known, so absolutely believed, that the retelling of them really wasn't necessary any longer. They simply said, "remember when . . . " then trailed off to nothing. And I thought that this was amazing. Because the impact of the feats of Pete the Clammer had indeed made him a legend, and in his lifetime, and he enjoyed it immensely. And for a long time he carried it very well. And he still doesn't carry it at all badly. And this is amazing also, considering its weight. But then people expect a hell of a lot from their legends, and they aren't always reasonable about it either. But for a long time it remained that the old men became certain that in youth they had been his equal, that they had bellied to the bar together. And it remained that the other commercial clammers knew all along that they could never be his equal, but they eagerly bellied to the bar with him anyway, to bask in the shine from his glow. And as a newcomer to the town, and to the waterfront, for all this focus and all this attention to be directed toward one man alone, was really a very special treat. And having Pete the Clammer alive and here and always daily among us, the old men and the young boys and the other clammers and me did not have the actual responsibility to become a legend, that we would have had if he were dead, or if he had never come here in the first place. But eventually, people do expect a hell of a lot from their legends.

Still, and again, time and place and circumstance and luck all have a great deal to do with the creation of a legend, and our legend was born and raised on Long Island. His father and his father, were commercial clammers. And quite naturally, their sons became commercial clammers. With the vast fertile areas of clam bottom in the bays and the sounds and the rivers around New York City, the fathers made a decent living from the water. As did the first of the sons. But Pete the Clammer was a much later son. And while the clam bottom areas remained vast and fertile, much of it was increasingly becoming polluted. So yearly, sometimes even monthly, a large tract here and a large tract there were withdrawn from the workable areas. This while more and more sons of commercial clammer fathers were becoming commercial clammers themselves. So as the size of the pie was decreasing, the number of those wanting a slice was increasing. And with shrinking slices, the much later sons really had to bust ass and hustle, just to make a fair living. But the people up there eat a whole lot of clams. And as the population continued to grow, so did the demand, and with this, the price paid per claim continued to rise. And for a while these rising prices almost kept up with the shrinking pie and the shrinking slices. But the handwriting was already boldly written on the wall for the much later sons to see. The pie was worth just so much, and it could be sliced just so many ways.

Pete the Clammer graduated high school. He preferred subjective courses to objective courses. He was good with his hands, and this led to his being a good worker. Before long, his assets included a-wife who was more cute than pretty, and two kids who were more rowdy than behaved. By then also, he had ragged long dark hair and a ragged full beard that tended to red in the sunlight. He had a ragged car and a ragged skiff and a ragged boat trailer. But he also had a good set of tongs, a good bullrake with both long and short handles, a good power rake, and a good hacking rack. And he had the excellent skills and the excellent instincts of several generations of commercial clammers, as well as the proper attitude for correctly applying these. In addition, though somewhat divergent, through self instruction, he had acquired an unusually sensitive knowledge of the complete works of Joseph Conrad and Jack London and Somerset Maugham that would cause a literary scholar to be envious. And it was with these various and assembled assets that Pete the Clammer started south, into the then unknown to him, in search of new clam bottom and the opportunities that would result from this.

The quehog, the hard clam, was known to habitat the entire east coast. Clamming the Chesapeake Bay, and farther south into Tideland Virginia had been a thriving industry for as long as it had been thriving around New York City, and therefore just as closed or closing. So any new clan bottom would have to be farther south still. In North Carolina, perhaps, or South Carolina, or Georgia, or even Florida. Wouldn't that be nice. And the word was that clams were truly thick in Florida. New York winters were miserably cold, ah but, Florida winters, yes, yes, they were beautifully warm. He would see. He would just begin, stopping to try here, stopping to try there, yes, he would see for himself. Because a commercial clammer must be an explorer also, if he is ever to become a top clammer. And Pete the Clammer certainly had the proper attitude to become a top clammer. Besides, he really didn't have much of a choice, what with the handwriting so boldly written on the wall there at home.

Hell, the Indians knew for five hundred years that the hundreds of miles of North Carolina coastline with its literal maze of rivers and bays and creeks and sounds was truly thick with clams. After all, didn't they have summer villages conveniently spaced all along the coastline to which to come every spring from inland for several months of sea and sun and seafood? That is until we killed off the ones of them that we couldn't drive off. Back then, under and in and above the sea was truly thick with everything. And the only thing that the coastline wasn't truly thick with was people. But by the time Pete the Clammer began his southward trek, all this was being reversed. And the North Carolina coastline had begun to be truly thick with people, while everything else had begun to be thin, and soon to be truly thin. But these people, these new Indians of a far different tribe, also had their conveniently spaced summer villages. And they, too, also came from inland every spring for several months of sea and sun and seafood. But remarkably, somehow the coastline was still truly thick with clams. Yes, and especially around Swansboro, especially here at the mouth of the White Oak River. Simply because no one as yet gave a damn about a clam. Oh they would! Yes hell they would! But not yet. Soon yes, but not yet. Because southerners have never been partial to clams as a seafood. A chowder now and then, yes, otherwise, no thank you sir. And besides eagerly minting their wampum from the shells, the original Indians weren't really too big on clams as a seafood either.

Somehow it is a seafood better suited to the colder climates, to the people with a permanent wind chill.

So with Pete the Clammer having begun his southward trek, the people of Swansboro could care less that the White Oak River was wall to wall like a carpet with clams, had they known it. Because no commercial fisherman here who was worth his salt, who was worthy of the name, would dare stoop to grovel for a lowly goddamn clam. No sir! No way! Not with the mullet and the shrimp and the spot and the trout and the scallop getting thin, but plenty thick still. Oh, the womenfolk and the kids might fart around and get a mess of clams of an evening now and then. But a commercial fisherman fart around in the muck and the mire for a goddamn clam?! Forget it! Absolutely! Because if the good Lord had meant for them to be clammers, He would have put a deadbolt in their ass to tie the clam tub string to. They did not have deadbolts in their asses, therefore, they did not clam. And a loud amen to that!

Then along comes Pete the Clammer, time and place and circumstance and luck having all come together. Ragged hair, ragged beard, cute wife and rowdy kids ragged too by then from the long trip, ragged car and ragged skiff. With his assembled clamming tools. Yes, these most certainly. But these never and not ever, ragged, no, not these tools so necessary to his trade. The bullrake. The mighty bullrake. Yes, especially the mighty bullrake. The bullrake is the most god awful looking contraption that you have ever seen or will ever see. And there are two stories of where it got its name. The first is that it bulls its way through the bottom. And this it does very well, almost too well, as it literally gouges off the top several inches of dead shells and mud and live clams and sand, the top layer of everything in its path. The second is that it takes a bull of a man to pull one. Of course commercial clammers prefer this version, and there is a lot of truth to it. But then, if a ten year old boy begins early to get the hang of pulling a bullrake, then he can pretty well keep with the men. As can a five foot tall dainty woman who has learned the subtleties of a bullrake. So the second version is more for the commercial clammers who are side by side bellied to the bar, as they very frequently are, who are already beer loud, and are soon to be even beer louder. But either version, the bullrake is still a god awful looking contraption. The pulling part is an aluminum tee handle, with the tee being not quite two feet wide, and the handle being adjusted to about seven feet long. At the end of the handle an upside down basket made from cold rolled steel rods has been tightly clamped. This basket is about a foot wide and a little more than two feet long. It is shaped like a high hump on an old lady's shoulders, with the hump slanting forward at a rather drastic angle. On the outside bottom edge of the basket, four inch long teeth made from tempered cold rolled steel have been welded at one inch intervals. These very sharp teeth slant down and back at the same drastic angle as the basket slants up and forward. It is these teeth that gouge the bottom and bull anything and everything into the collector basket as the bullrake is pulled along with short, strong, controlled strokes. Now is that a god awful looking contraption, or is that a god awful looking contraption!

So again, with time and place and circumstance and luck having all come together, along comes Pete the Clammer to Swansboro with one. Well, the fishermen here had never seen one. They had never even heard of one. And now seeing one, they asked, "What the hell is that god awful looking contraption?" To which Pete the Clammer proudly replied, "That's a bullrake." Well sir, the fishermen looked from Pete the Clammer, to the bullrake, back to Pete the Clammer raggedly standing there, then back to the bullrake. "What does it do?" asked they in complete puzzlement, while seriously doubting that it could do anything except sit there and look god awful. "Digs clams," was Pete the Clammer's proud announcement. "Are you shitting me!" hollered they in surprised disbelief, in a unison chorus, with this immediately followed by a suitably hearty long round of gaaroffs and scoffs, as hard hands slapped thighs in wild merriment, after which followed real choking paashaws and spitting chorckles, that ended with breathless gasping shizzes and teary bleary eyes, and the wet blowing of runny full noses." "Ah shit, that's rich. Digs clams. Ah shit. Whheeww."

When the present day Indians of that far different tribe come to the coast in the spring for their several months of sea and sun and seafood, the bald top husbands precisely steer their gutturally

If it had existed, it would still exist. Since it no longer exists, then it never existed. So there!

But trust me, well, humor me at least, while I strongly plead that though their refuge is indeed quickly out of sight there below the surface, it assuredly has not vanished. Because, yes Virginia, there really is a bottom there beneath all that water. And their tossed refuge will lie as ugly litter upon this bottom for the very long length of its plastic existence, that in even more frequent trails is being imposed upon this another inner world that is within our larger world. Because the bottom of this another world has a truly spectacular natural scenic panorama that broadly spans from deep grass valleys to barren dull deserts, and all the stunningly fascinating variety that is in between. There are rolling hill plains here, and craggy mountain ranges here. There are black chism holes here, and white slanted shoals here, here in this another world. There are mushy mud bottoms where the mud is so fluffy that it is almost suspended. Here in this another world, there are dense sand bottoms where the sand is so hard that it is almost indestructible. And the rocky reefs that are so abundantly positioned about the bottom of this another world in grand curving arcs, in blunt buttresses, in raised platforms, in bumpy depressions, are the careful result of a thousand years collection of the dead shelled sea animals whose empty and whose broken homes the ever shifting and the always changing tides have slowly gathered and have gradually compacted into continuing communities and towns and cities. Oysters, whelks, clams, scallops, snails, the long list, these gathered shells, these compacted shells, these shells

shells shells. These shells that are the living graveyards of this another world. These thriving, growing, and so vibrant graveyards. Because it is to these broken dead shells that the vulnerable spawn of another generation of shelled sea animals attach themselves so they will not be swept away and be so exposed and be so available to their many many predators. And it is within the roughly scarred surfaces of these rocky reefs that the hard clam, the quehog, so prospers and so multiplies, also. The various dead providing a sheltered home for the various new living. The endless cycle recycling itself endlessly.

So it was to the rocky reefs, the rocks as commercial clammers call them, that Pete the Clammer first went in his skiff with that god awful looking contraption. Because he knew that the rocks would be where the clams would be the most concentrated, and therefore the more quickly harvested. But not before checking with the local fish house owner to be certain that he would have a buyer for them. Because just as actors and writers and professional athletes cannot even begin to be launched without having an agent, so too commercial fishermen cannot even untie from the dock without having a buyer. And just as with agents, a fish house owner must be a man apart also. A man who most definitely has a galloping god complex. Because here, as in all fishing villages, the seafood buyer is indeed the literal local god. And the poverty level rises and falls with the arbitrary prices that he pays. When the buyer is feeling especially benevolent, the poverty eases somewhat for the duration of that mood. But people who are not hungry cannot be dominated. So the buyer can be only so benevolent, and benevolent for only so long. So commercial fishermen have come to know these four truths: that the sun will come up, that the tide will turn, that the wind will blow, and that before the sun goes down the seafood buyer will screw him. And not just a wham bam thank you ma'am quickly screwing either. But a real rattle the windows, wake the kids, breakdown the bed, reaming out screwing.

And when the buyer has settled back for a cigarette, it will be without a kiss, or a hug, or even a see you later baby pat on the fanny. And when the fisherman's wife snuggles to him in the night, he will say, "sorry dear, I gave at the office." Because the professors at the agent colleges are all retired fish house owners. Because what the hell can a commercial fisherman do with five hundred pounds of croaker, or fifth bushels of scallops, or three hundred pounds of shrimp? He can eat seafood until his shit turns to seaweed, and still not dent a corner of his catch. If he holds his catch for more than a day, all he has is a huge rotting stink. And the light company and the grocery store and the landlord won't cash seafood. Because barter ain't legal tender around here no more. So the fisherman must convert his catch, and each day, he simply does not have any other choice. So his friendly local buyer is indeed and in fact, more god than God himself.

So when Pete the Clammer asked if he would buy his clams, the fish house owner said sure, at four cents. He normally paid three cents a clam, but what the hell. This ragged yankee with the still ragged from the long trip wife and kids was obviously down and out, or else he wouldn't be here in Swansboro in the first place, and especially here in Swansboro clamming. Clamming of all things, and with that god awful looking contraption, when all the real commercial fishermen were scalloping or fishing or shrimping. But then, the fish house owner couldn't lose, he simply could not. Because just for grading by size and counting and bagging the clams, and tossing the bags into the back of his pick me up truck, then driving to the wholesaler in Baltimore, he would double his money. Just as he doubled his money on the other seafood also. So what the hell, he'd pay this ragged yankee a penny more. No one came in with over several hundred clams anyway, and they went to Baltimore along with everything else. No swinging load, nothing special, no big deal. But then this is the fish house owner's private secret. Because all he needs is some cash, any kind of a dock, any kind of a building with a cooler, and a pick me up truck. And he can double his money in Baltimore. That secret, that so simple secret, his private secret. Everyone else did the work, he made the profit. One hell of a secret, this god's secret.

So Pete the Clammer cranked his outboard, then away he and his skiff went from the dock, under the two highway bridges to Morehead City, and up the White Oak River. Heading for a rock, the first rock, the last rock, any rock in between, searching for clams to bullrake. The fishermen there lined at the dock, still winding down their whizzing and blowing. "Dig clams. Ah shit. Whheeww." But came evening, and, Katy bar the door, grab your ass and run, hold her Luke she's heading for the barn, in chugs Pete the Clammer, his skiff so low in the water she's taking seas, him steering with one hand and bailing like hell with the other hand. Until finally tied to the dock, and lo and behold his skiff is almost crowned over the clams, with Pete the Clammer knee deep in clams. With the fishermen's bursting chorus ricocheting along the dock, and both ways on the waterfront too, "wher'in the almighty hell you get them??!" With Pete the Clammer's quiet reply, "up river." With that skiff load being the most clams seen in one place around here, ever, absolutely ever. And a swinging skiff load it was, for certain, for sure. And when the load was finally counted, the count came to more than five thousand clams. "What! Say What?! Five Thousand Clams! Five Ever Loving Thousand God Damn Clams! You Mean To Tell Me That This Here Ragged Assed Yankee Kid Got Five God Damn Thousand Ever Loving Clams In One Day?! In One Day! And With That There Contraption?! Naw! No Way!" Well sir, at four cents a clam, you're talking about more than two hundred dollars for one day's work, at a time when one hundred dollars for one day's work at any kind of commercial fishing, even as mate on a big trawler, was extraordinary. And from clams! From clams! Clams of all things. Why no one clams. Least of all a real commercial fisherman. From clams! With the wet sniffling having stopped. With the whheewwing having stopped. With the gaarroffs and the chorckles having stopped. With the disbelief and the complete amazement then shifting to offense. "Just who'in the hell does that god damn yankee kid think he is coming down here with that contraption and getting our clams?!" With offense then shifting to defense. "Well, we knowed they was out there all along, just ain't had time to go get 'um." Defense then having run its course, became grudging respect. "Still, that's one hell of a kid, that ragged assed kid there is." And so it was on that day that Pete the Clammer got the only name that he would ever have around here. Pete the Clammer. Pete the Clammer, the one who introduced the bullrake to Swansboro. Pete the Clammer, the one who got five thousand clams his first day out. Pete the Clammer, the Legend.

The only time that commercial clammers will ever set high fashion styling is if saltwater crusted sloppy suddenly becomes the craze. And don't hold your breath waiting for that. But then, nothing lasts for very long around saltwater. Not men, not metals, and certainly not clothing. So none of us really gives much thought to what we wear. All we ask is that it at least last for a while before it becomes absolutely too torn to wear. And if it does last, then who cares how it looks or whether it fits or whether it is coordinated? After all, the clams don't care. The wind doesn't care either, and the tides don't care, and Pete the Clammer certainly doesn't care. In fact, he is the attire model that most of us copied from. He appears tall at first look, but this is more lankiness that tallness. But he would still wall measure a little over six feet, that is if he stood up straight. The drab frayed trousers that he always wears droop badly in the rear and they just barely cling to too narrow hips. He is especially partial to worn holey tee shirts, with an unbuttoned, faded and floppy long sleeve flannel shirt worn over them. The flannel shirts would hang better if he didn't slouch, which he does, which is just bad posture caused by laziness. But he does slouch, but he certainly doesn't care about this either, so what can you do? You can't scold a grown man. But what the hell, this ain't no biggy, and since Pete the Clammer cares less, right away you begin to care less. Because people have always willingly adapted to his easy personality. His shoulders are a little broad, but not really broad. And his biceps are a little muscular, but not really muscular. Both of which are somewhat surprising for a man who has had to constantly use his upper body strength for hard manual labor for most of his life. At first look you notice also that his arms are really a little too long for his height. And for a time this is puzzling. Then you realize that your arms would be stretched a little too, if you had gripped and pulled and snatched and jerked and heavy lifted a bullrake every day and all day for year after year.

If you ever visit Swansboro, and on a whim of daring decide to stand side by side tall with that times' bullraker crowd loud talking at the bar at the Jolly Roger, while calming your reluctance at being so closely surrounded by so rough and tumble a group, it will be their hands that will provide you with your strongest and your longest lasting impression. And wherever you may go from there, and however much time might pass since then, you will be able to right away identify a bullraker from across a room just by his hands, however he may be dressed, and whatever his profession might be at that time. But if you fail to notice his hands beforehand, then his slow and firm and sure handshake will be as good a give away as any. And having been out there at it earlier and later and with a far better attitude than the rest of us, Pete the Clammer's hands are exaggerations of the hands of all bullrakers, past and present and future. His fingers are long and sinuey, and they look stretched just as his arms look stretched. But his palms are definitely muscular, and they are thickly calloused with meaty pads, and they are wider and flatter than any palms that you have ever seen. The skin on his hands is creased and cracked and dry and cut and chafed, and the skin is seawater slick and it is sun baked shiny. Patches of white scaly permanent sun poisoning, break out, heal over, then move to another place on his hands. But it is the unnatural curl, of Pete the Clammer's hands, that is the universal curl of all bullraker's hands. Because once having seriously pulled a bullrake in making a living as a commercial clammer, his hands, and our hands, will always be pulling a bullrake, while idle, even in repose.

The next afternoon Pete the Clammer wallowed to the dock with another taking seas over the gunnels swinging skiff load of clams. And the next afternoon. So it was during this time that he really became the talk of Swansboro, the rage of Swansboro, even the toast of Swansboro. And wherever he went in town, people would stop and point him out and say to anyone nearby, "There's Pete the Clammer. He brought the bullrake to Swansboro, and got five thousand clams his first day out." Because only in a commercial fishing town do they understand that to beat the sea at anything is an accomplishment. Because the sea isn't often beaten, and she certainly isn't beaten consistently. So however it may be done, at whatever type of fishing, the townspeople realized that only a man could do it. So with the legend of Pete the Clammer having been begun, then it could only spread. And the farther it spread, and the more often that it was retold, then the bigger and better it became, until now you can no longer separate the fact of the legend from the fiction of the legend. But fact or fiction, it is still a damn good story. And Pete the Clammer thoroughly enjoyed this new fame, this new found acclaim. He had found a home here, he would travel no more. It would be in Swansboro that he would remain. So he rented a house with plans of one day buying it, and he and his cute wife and his just a little rowdy kids settled in. And with his bringing home far more money than they had hoped for, had ever even dreamed of, it seemed as though it would be a pretty good life indeed. Long Island would become a place for them to look back upon. Long Island would be just a place that they visited once a year.

And if Pete the Clammer could do this well clamming, then the young fishermen of Swansboro were sure that they could do at least half as well, even though they had never before pulled a bullrake. But with that much money at stake, they could learn, and they certainly would learn. And half as well was still not bad money at all. So, like children awaiting for Christmas, for the next week a swinging load of new bullrakes ordered from Long Island couldn't get to Swansboro by truck fast enough. And during the week that followed many of these student bullrakers were actually bringing in several thousand clams a day. Because it is surprising how quickly a person can learn a skill that reduces hunger. And with the bonanza having begun, the bonanza was off and running and gaining momentum daily, and there wasn't any stopping it now. So the fish house owner promptly dropped his price from four cents to three cents, and was seriously considering two cents. Not because his costs had risen, or because his selling price had dropped, rather because as the only clam buyer in town he had a monopoly on this new gravy train, and who more than he deserved to ride this train for all that it was worth? But the bullrakers didn't complain much more than a few brief grumbles, because they were still awash in money. Because clams had suddenly brought prosperity to Swansboro. Because Pete the Clammer had suddenly brought prosperity to Swansboro. And rather than guarding his skills, his keys to the goldfield, Pete the Clammer shared them openly and equally with all as though this bonanza were something that they now had in common, their bond for the future, a craftsman quickly assembling a guild of new craftsmen. He eagerly showed them the hows and the whys and the whens and the wheres of proper bullraking. He endlessly described the characteristics as well as the peculiarities of the quehog. And in the evenings they bellied as a group to the bar at the Jolly Roger, with Pete the Clammer three deep surrounded by his excited to learn and anxious to do better students. And within minutes the air in there was absolutely thick with their loud talk and their cigarette smoke, and the zesty fragrance of foamy beer. As well as the so sweet smell of sweat and seawater and clams, and most of all, money. Ah yes, money, money. Because prosperity had suddenly come to the Jolly Roger also.

And everywhere Pete the Clammer went during these early years, he was glad that he had gone. Because everyone wanted to meet him. Because everyone wanted to talk with him. Because everyone wanted to be seen with him. Because everyone wanted to buy Pete the Clammer a beer. And he thoroughly enjoyed the crowds and the bars and the talk, and the beers and the attention and the friendship. He had indeed found a home here. And on the yearly visits to Long Island, he told widely and long of the wondrous town that was Swansboro. Of its wondrous year around weather. Of its wondrous clamming, and of its wondrous people.

Any many of the young bullrakers there heard and heeded, and immediately began to pack in order to start south. There not being any kind of clamming future for them in Long Island. There being a truly amazing clamming future for them in Swansboro. And everywhere Pete the Clammer went, he was glad that he had gone. But his cute wife only wanted him home in the evenings, for herself, for the kids, for their future. And by now she had gotten pretty damn well fed up with this whole celebrity business. Because Pete the Clammer had settled into the routine of being on the water most of the day, and in the bars most of the night. And when he did finally get home, he could only stumble through the door, then crash into oblivion on the couch. Certainly there must have been quiet discussions which led to full blown arguments. Certainly there must have been gentle urgings which led to harsh threats. But unlike the beginning to troop south Long Island bullrakers, Pete the Clammer did not hear and he did not heed. Because one night his couch crashing into oblivion had a pronounced echo to it. Because his cute wife had upped and gone. Cute wife gone, just a little rowdy kids gone, home gone. Only the rented house remained. Only silence remained. Silence, and the seed of what would quickly become a wild and contorted resentment that approached hatred toward women. Any woman, all women, ex-cute wife especially, and in particular. But the crowds were still here, and the beer, and the buddies. So everywhere Pete the Clammer went during the next years, he was still glad that he had gone.

And through it all he went on laughing his good laugh, to quiet the hurt and to span the loss. To rustle the silence and to dim the resentment, that matured anyway in spite of the laughter. Still laughing his good laugh that was his happy present to all. The laugh that could easily be heard a mile across the water even against a stiff headwind, so that we who were scattered and solitary and visible only as tiny figures beside small boats would look up at the first laughter roll and smile and say aloud to our lonely out there selves, "There's Pete the Clammer over there," and then the loneliness wasn't as huge. The good laugh that always made new friends from a moment ago strangers wherever he went. Because just the hearing of it caused others to also smile, then to chuckle and to laugh along in a broadening chorus that gained and grew. It is a strong laugh and a caring laugh and a bold laugh. And it begins so low and rumbles deep, then reverberates all about until it spirals out. Then expands fast and wider and larger like the quick wave swells traveling from a rock tossed in water. It is a fine laugh and a fun laugh, and it is a man's laugh indeed. Because when Pete the Clammer laughs everything becomes better and everyone becomes brighter. And the mood lightens and the attitudes soften. And the tempers cool and the frustrations thin. And cloudy weather becomes sunny and warm. And his laugh is as much a part of his legend as anything else.

It was during these years that the Indians of that far different tribe began to discover Swansboro and the near by beaches at

Emerald Isle. Just as others of them were discovering other villages and other beaches all along the coast of North Carolina. This began as a trickle, innocent enough and happy enough and welcome enough, with the locals gradually building restaurants and shops and motels to accommodate and to entertain these summer visitors. And the break from total dependence upon commercial fishing was refreshing, and the new jobs and the new money and the new acquaintances were invigorating. But it didn't take many years though for the trickle to become a steady stream that became a cascading river, that then brought with it land use problems and zoning problems and utility problems and pollution problems and traffic problems. And with the cascading river increasingly annually and in real earnest, and apparently without there being a limit or an end to it, then suddenly all the many problems became more complex and more costly and more permanent. But for a long while back then, having the summer visitors was just pleasant. And it was nice to watch them appreciate for several weeks, for several months, the everywhere around natural beauty that we had to enjoy all year. And in the new bars and in the new restaurants and in the new lounges, these new Indians discovered Pete the Clammer also. Because, if it was almost impossible for him to get home early when his cute wife and his just a little rowdy kids were there, then he sure as hell wasn't going home early when only echoing silence was there. So these bars and restaurants and lounges became his home, and the rented house became where he went to shower after clamming, where he went to change clothes before clamming, where sometimes he even went to sleep.

But these new Indians are like the smoothly rounded stones of a mountain creek bed. And they are very unlike the jagged outcropping of an ocean inlet. Because it is always confining where they come from, and the contact that they have among themselves is as wearing as it is constant. Until, like anything that has been uniformed, there is very little variation among the members of each group, just as there is very little variation among the members of separate groups. So when you have seen one of these new Indians, then you have seen all of these new Indians. But most of all they dislike for argument or self or belligerence or radicalism or confrontation to disrupt the smooth flow of their smooth lives. And while they normally avoid these disruptions decisively, strangely, they saw in Pete the Clammer something lost but familiar, something old but irresistible, as though his truly rough edges reminded them of what they had been and no longer were, and never could be again. Because here was a man who had left everything safe behind to go to a different place to do a far different type of work that few men could do or would do and do this work against elements that if not dangerous, certainly were frequently hazardous, and to immediately be a pioneer and an innovator at this different work so that he became more successful at it than any man before or since around here. So they had found Pete the Clammer, a free man, an uncomplicated man, an exciting man, a man who could do absolutely as he chose, go as he chose, dress as he chose, speak as he chose, and believe absolutely as he chose. They had found the last true individual, the everything that secretly they thought of themselves as. And for a long while they thought of him as splendid indeed. So the bald top men and the perfectly pretty women pulled him into their uniform lives to share with him their valuable smooth time. After all, could he not discuss at length and in depth the complete works of Jack London and Joseph Conrad and Somerset Maugham with great sensitivity, and did he not do pencil portraits of them now and then while exaggerating their warts only hilariously? And could he not tell of the real sea and its animals and its potentials and its whims in a fascinating way that somehow was beyond them? They had never before met such a man, they had never before met such an individual, and they were sure that they never would again. So they competed among themselves for this legend to share their tables, share their food and drink, share their time and their precious friendship also. While the delicate handed men continually readjusted the inside climate, and the seemingly serenely indifferent women silently pondered their large woolly itches. And wherever Pete the Clammer went, he was glad that he had gone.

There are some clams wherever there is saltwater along the entire east coast. But there are thick populations of clams only in those special places where everything required is well balanced. And from the two highway bridges that go to Morehead City, here at the mouth of the White Oak River, for two miles upriver and for a mile across, everything is certainly well balanced. There is enough tide to provide good regular flushes, while still maintaining high salinity. Too little tide and the salinity will remain either too high or too low, and fresh plankton cannot be brought in frequently enough for the clams to feed well and to grow quickly, and the spawn will not be scattered widely enough for the clams to have sufficient room. Too much tide and the flush will be too drastic for such casual and fattening feeding, and the spawn will be swept away before it can safely attach itself to anything. But here at the mouth of the White Oak River everything is well balanced. Good flushing tides, together with seasons that are extreme just enough, produce clams that are fat and salty and hearty and have a good shelf life. Man's machines could never balance anything so well, and the long term value of an area such as this for its renewable resource is great. But any North Carolina resident with several bucks for a license can harvest clams here without restrictions.

When Pete the Clammer first went out to clam the White Oak, the clam population was so thick, so truly dense, in the rocks and in the shelly places, that the very sharp teeth of his bullrake could not dig into the bottom. So he had to walk around and to literally stomp down the bullrake basket to crush and to move aside enough clams so the teeth could dig in. And when he walked in the sandy places with few shells, it was like walking on a broad apron of small cobblestones, the clams were that dense. It was absolutely amazing. And with such perfect balance, with such continual renewability, this area alone could have provided work for forty full time commercial clammers and three clam buyers. It could have been a never ending local industry that well supported the forty clammers and the buyers and their employees families that resulted. But any North Carolina resident with several bucks for a license can harvest as many clams as he can find, even if they are the last two clams, without restrictions.

Still, Pete the Clammer and a hell of a lot of other clammers made damn good money for a lot of years before the resource simply could no longer withstand such constant pressure from so many harvesters. Because by now a number of Long Island clammers were already down and settled in and working regularly, with several more coming down each year. Until the sound of yankee voices had become as common around here as the sight of tongs and bullrakes and long handles and pearakes and power rakes in the boats at the docks all along the waterfront. And more and more of the local young commercial fishermen had become converted hardcore clammers. And never again did anyone make the wisecrack that if the good lord had wanted him to clam he would have put a deadbolt in his ass. Even the older retired fishermen and other local retirees were, and seemingly everyone in Swansboro was, out on the water in a wild and a frantic search for what only several years before they didn't even know existed, and if they had of known, wouldn't have farted with on a bet. "Me clam? Me? Get out of Here!" Yep, it really was a bonanza, and it was a gold rush. And it was like going out and picking up money in the street. Because at low tide, by carefully following the adjoining sandbars, you can walk almost a mile up river from the two highway bridges. So even housewives with kids in their arms and kids trailing behind had begun to go out and hand clam fill their largest laundry basket in an inner tube that they and the kids could drag in when full. And there were many days now when you could almost walk across the White Oak just by stepping from one anchored boat to another anchored to another anchored boat to another. It was

103

amazing alright, and it staggered the imagination, and it was obscene. Because you really didn't have to be a commercial clammer to find plenty of clams. No experience, no special skill or knowledge, simply stop your boat wherever the mood struck, get overboard and begin, and before long you had all the clams that you wanted to mess with. Because a bunch of clams get mighty heavy mighty fast, and they are bulky and hard to handle. And it wasn't long before everyone was loudly bitching because they had to lift and shift and move about this weighty money before they could get it to the buyer. Because it all was so easy. Because it all was too easy. Even farmers and carpenters and pulpwood workers and gas station mechanics from as far away as one hundred miles inland were packing up the wife and kids and grandma too into their pick me up trucks to come here to hand clam on weekends on all fours in the sandy mud and grass of the many shallow small bays and creeks and sloughs that are scattered one leading to another from Swansboro to the ocean. Until everywhere you looked, it looked like a gigantic crop of heads and washtubs had been planted in the water, and the crop was ripe. Heads and washtubs, heads and washtubs. Heads and washtubs wherever you looked, heads and washtubs everywhere. Yep, it really was a bonanza, and it was a gold rush. And it was like going out and picking up money in the street. It was amazing alright, and it staggered the imagination, and it was obscene.

And just as clammers and clamming equipment and rapid Long Island speech have become usual around Swansboro now, so too, the Indians of that far different have become usual. So usual in fact that somehow and when no one was looking these new Indians have so invaded and occupied and multiplied that they have actually become the new Swansboro. And the dwindling old timers can only stand bewildered and worriedly scratch their heads and wonder when this transference and ultimate deposition happened. And they can only huddle defensively within the shrinking circle of their quaint homes and hurriedly discuss a historical district for the town and historical preservation for its buildings as their only counterattack. And they can only cherish among themselves what had been and who had been and how it had been before the clam went the way of the fish and the shrimp and the crab. Now that nothing can ever again be as it was, now that the new Indians are especially fascinated by quaintness. And they purchase all of it that comes available, anywhere and anytime, and at any price, as though this end alone were beyond a goal and beyond as obsession, and were truly a matter of life or death to them. But strangely, and even mysteriously, the purchased quaintness soon fades then vanishes all together under their ownership and with their handling, and what results is a transplanted uniformity that is exactly like whichever inland place that they came from. Until quaintness also now has begun to go the way of everything else. And while some of them are busy buying Swansboro, others of them are busy buying ocean front condos as fast as the once high dunes can be leveled and the glass structures raised. Because they are indeed busy, and they are ambitious, and they are not easily distracted. But the more frantically that they seek difference, the more certain it is that the results will be duplication. And now that they have bought almost all of the prime ocean front property and the inshore waterfront property, they are rushing to buy all of the tidal marshland property, as though this too were equally as precious and equally as expendable. And this property too is being resold among themselves faster than it can be drained and filled and subdivided. And in the early years when the old timers lacked the enthusiasm and the capital with which to run this race toward this wild massive sprawling buying boom, these new Indians were eagerly waiting, and heavily loaded both with enthusiasm and with capital. Because, yes they really are busy, and yes they really are ambitious, and no they are not easily distracted. So they have built antique shops and bookstores and beachwear shops. And they have built seafood shoppes and convenience stores and amusement parks. Because they will build anything that will reduce the money of the others of them.

They came as summer visitors, but they have stayed to become permanent landlords. And uniformity has followed them wherever they have gone. Until the contact here has become as constant and as wearing and as confining as it is inland. Until now there are mostly only smooth rounded stones here also. The jagged outcroppings having almost all gone the way of everything else. Because they do consider appearance as so very necessary, as so very important. And the restaurants and the lounges that they built, that would have gone bankrupt especially during the long cold winters of their first struggling and establishing years if it had not been for the patronage of the clammers and the other fishermen, gradually and now firmly no longer tolerate or will even admit so rowdy and so smelly and so sloppily dressed and so crude a collection of men. We were a godsend, now we are just bad for business. We were a large part of the original quaintness, now we are just a detriment to proper appearance. Because with prosperity, comes order, and with order, then control must follow. So the Riptide, that always was on the wrong side of the two highway bridges, has become a cleared lot that waits for a marina expansion. And the Porthole, that always was just a brawl about to happen, has become a fashionable gift shoppe that is perfumed with dignity. But somehow the Jolly Roger has so far endured as the fishermen's sanctuary that it has always been. And most days now, Pete the Clammer is at the Jolly by two in the afternoon so as not to crowd too closely the midnight closing.

And he is still pretty much the same Pete the Clammer who had come to Swansboro as a bold young man so many years ago. Though some grey has come to his hair now, and some lines have come in his face now, and his boldness having become a lot more quiet now. And not nearly as adventurous now, his having kicked back and relaxed and comfortably settled into this place and these times and these people, his one great adventure having been broadly enacted. But still long haired and still full bearded and still ragged with the open long sleeved shirts worn loose and flapping over torn tee shirts. Still outgoing and fun and funny and easy to talk with about many subjects, and still very much seawater world knowledgeable. And still laughing, yes, most of all and best of all, still laughing that good laugh, his good laugh. But only rarely now clammer, and far less capable clammers regularly top him, his body having slowed as his spirit dwindled as his attitude thinned. But then, nothing lasts for very long around saltwater. Not woods, not metals, not clothing, and certainly not men. It is the constant wind and the constant weather and the constant exposure to both that so drains physically and so frays emotionally. It is the so hard labor of endless days and endless months and endless years of lifting and pulling and carrying and jerking. It is the harsh awareness of sun and tides and storm fronts and winds shifts, the sharp attention to danger and the careful prevention of harm. It is about always having to worry about fluctuating clam prices, and about always trying to outsmart the cheating buyers, and about always having to find clams tomorrow. And it is about keeping the bills paid and keeping some structure to your life, and about always maintaining your skiff and your outboard motor and your clamming equipment. Because you are entirely alone when you work on the water. and you and only you are responsible, and you and only you have to do the all and the everything that has to be done that must be done. Until finally it seems as though it is you and only you against the world and against all odds. This while it is still very much a young man's work and very much a young man's workplace, where only the strong and the sturdy can withstand it before gradually then suddenly it breaks them too just as it finally breaks all of us.

So, yes, Pete the Clammer has slowed a lot, has slackened quite a bit these days, and usually all he wants to do now is to get by and to enjoy his beer and his friends and to talk about the old days and about what he has done. He farted around with working a line of crab pots for a time. He farted around with building wooden work skiffs for a time. He farted around with shrimping and scalloping and oystering for a time. He farted around with working a line of eel pots for a time. He farted around with smoking fish for a time. Right now he is farting around with throw net catching live bait and keeping them in holding tanks to sell to the sports fishermen at tournament time when they will pay anything for anything that wiggles. And several months from now you can be sure that he will be farting around with something else. Because he has become very good at farting around, and after almost a lifetime of working on the water, farting around on the water is about the only fun left in working on the water. But if he is ever again of a mind, and if he ever again adjusted his attitude accordingly, then he could find a thousand clams in a bottom where no one else could find a hundred clams. Because after everything has been said and after everything has been done, he is still Pete the Clammer, the Legend, and however much his body might slow and his spirit might dwindle, that fact alone can never be changed. Because he has always been Pete the Clammer, the Legend, and he will always be Pete the Clammer, the Legend. But he really doesn't like to be ass deep in seawater anymore. And after all of these years of being ass deep in seawater, seawater itself has come to truly bother him. And only another long time commercial clammer can understand how this thing that once so compelled him, that once so mesmerized him, that once so filled so completely and so lovingly all of his days, now has become the one thing and the single most thing that he dreads and that he fears and that he avoids, while still and not ever being able to stay for very long away from its sight and its smell and its touch.

But people expect a hell of a lot from their legends. Because so few people ever venture far from the safety of the crowd. Because so few people ever take real risks for fear that they will fail. Because so many people are afraid to stand alone because of the loneliness that is there. So when a rare man does rise to stand full length above and beyond the rest, and accepts the risks and the loneliness and ignores the safety, then people look up to him and they come to expect and even demand that he go on even farther and become the everything that they are not and that they can never be. So by the time the once vast clam population up the White Oak River above the two highway bridges and around Swansboro to the sea had been thinned until it was nearly naked then rethinned until it approached extinction by the many years of unrestricted harvesting by the army of clammers, when five hundred clams a day had become a really good day and five thousand clams a day a long ago distant memory, then the people expected that Pete the Clammer would have gone on to other high conquests that were at other far heights. They expected him to have begun another clam gold rush in South Carolina, or in Georgia, or in Florida even. Or Alaska! Yeah! Now that would have been truly fitting to them, for Pete the Clammer to have gone on and begun a clam gold rush in Alaska. Or they expected him to have become the most successful and the most considerate and the most innovative clam buyer in Swansboro, then North Carolina, then all along the East Coast. Or they expected him to have opened a clam and oyster restaurant in Swansboro that led to a sprawling across the country chain of Pete the Clammer Restaurants. Or they expected him to have a acquired a small trawler that had led to a whole worldwide fleet of really big trawlers. Yeah, the people expected a hell of a lot from Peter the Clammer. At the very least, they expected something from him. Anything, but something, at the very least. But what they got was just a gradually getting older version of the same Pete the Clammer, who stubbornly continued to clam the same bottom, the same bays, the same rocks, in the same ways, in the same skiff, whose daily totals had slowly shrunk then finally dwindled to a pitiful fraction of what his daily totals had been. Who had begun to fart around with many things in order to avoid becoming once again dedicated to one thing.

So the new Indians were not distracted by Pete the Clammer for very long, they being far too ambitious and far too busy for someone who is not always entertaining. Because it is not enough for them to be only amused, they must also be entertained, before they will pound your back and buy your drinks and embrace you into their world as friend for any length of time. But their demanding hunger for always entertainment is very consuming, and that is why their candidate list of entertaining acquaintances is in a constant state of addition and subtraction and revision according to degree. Because to them, boredom, unlike property taxes, can be absolutely avoided. And when others have the responsibility of always entertaining you, then it is not necessary for you to ever have to confront your personal self while entertaining yourself.

For the rest of us, though, our disappointment with Pete the Clammer remained mild, and it never became hurtful, and to us it really did not detract from his legend or from our support of that. It simply was like a great musician who settles for being only a good musician, rather than ever becoming a songwriter, and by so doing the public's anticipation of his quest just dims a bit. Because after all, an adventure is far more exciting the higher and farther that it travels. But if an adventure is only briefly high and far exciting, then that is what you accept to be what you have to remember. Because in reality much in life is being content with the best that comes your way, and with whatever portion that it is measured in.

Because commercial clammers are the least reliable of men, and predictable only in so far as our stubborness approaches and usually achieves hardheadedness. We are extremely independent, or else we could not do this work that requires so much self-sufficiency. Since the work is all repetition, we must be able to dull our brains for the six to eight hours everyday, or else we could not withstand the endless monotony. Since the work is done alone, with each silently gathering our pay clam by clam slowly, we must be able to endure solitude. Since the work requires stamina and endurance above all, we must have a high threshold of pain. And a good head for business, and the diversity and the flexibility that this demands, is really not necessary, and in fact it can be a deterrent. The commercial clammer must have more hope than plan, more scheme than detail, and we must be more explorer than builder, more pioneer than homesteader. And for a lot of years, Pete the Clammer imminently filled all these requirements and he certainly was well qualified. Because he was the first of the first. Because he was the best of the best. Because he introduced the bullrake to Swansboro. Because he got five thousand clams his first day out. And by doing all these he became a legend in his own time. This at the hardest of work. This at the harshest of labor. This while those who feel cheated by him have not lived nor will ever live the procession of brutally cold winters that are always closely followed by dizzingly hot summers. Nor have they ever been stranded way out in a tiny skiff upon the big water during thunderstorm or fog or gale. Nor will they have to live the rest of their lives with enlarged hands or with swollen elbow joints that will remain permanently damaged. Nor will they have a fixed squint, or have weathered tough skin that is deeply wind scarred and is badly sun splotched. And they will not ever dream the reoccurring terrible dream of the monsters that really do not reside in the sea.

So enjoy yourself, Pete the Clammer. So live your life, Pete the Clammer. Because you have already accomplished far more than most. Yessir!, far far more than most.

FOR ONLY ME

She was just another woman who worked as a waitress at the seafood restaurant for tourists that is along the waterfront here in our town. I was just another man who worked as a commercial fisherman on the rivers and the bays and the sounds that are everywhere all around here. She worked nights and I worked days and it was rarely and in passing that we saw each other.

One morning a year or more ago as I was about to go down to my boat, she came to the apartment house where I rent to inquire about a vacancy. The landlord was not there right then, so I told her as much as I knew about the vacant apartment. That was the first time I had seen her. We stood at my door and we talked for awhile, and right away I really liked her smile. It was a very personal way of smiling that she had. And it was a warm smile and an easy smile, and I thought, a for only me smile. And I thought that she was quite attracted to me also, or else she would not smile at me in that very personal way. But even though the apartment rent was rather inexpensive, she said that she had just started to work at the restaurant and that it was more than she could afford. That she would continue staying at the rooming house. So I stood at my door and I watched her walk back toward what little there is of our downtown that is along the waterfront. And I very much wanted to make love to her. But for the life of me I could not remember what she had said her name was.

When you harvest some sort of seafood everyday, you do not care to eat seafood all that often. But to the few inland friends of mine who now and then come here to visit, eating seafood is a big treat, and therefore is the first thing that they want to do. So I take them to the tourist restaurant and they thoroughly enjoy their meal as though this alone makes their visit worthwhile. It is a large restaurant and many women work as waitresses there. So it is not unusual that there has not been a time during the past year that the woman whose name I could not remember was our waitress. But at sometime during these my infrequent nights out she would pass close by our table on her way from her tables to the kitchen or returning from it. And as soon as she recognized me she would smile her warm and easy and for only me smile. And always and right away and again, I very much wanted to make love to her.

The young men who are commercial fishermen here are still resilient enough to bounce back quickly from the hard manual labor and the constant exposure to every weather that we endure. But I am no longer that resilient, and I come down rather hard after my long day on the water. So the few beers that I now and then have in the evening at the bar with the other fishermen have a profound affect upon me, as I quickly go from quite talkative and excited about the day, to simply tired and hungry and without very much to say. Lately I have been coming to the bar more often because I have been scalloping on a boat with two other guys. And when we have docked our catch and have been paid the lump sum for it, it is natural that we would come to the bar to discuss the day and to plan tomorrow and to divide the money. And lately also, the waitress has been off work more often because the restaurant has temporarily cut back from six nights a week to weekend nights during these the worst winter months because just a few tourists come here now. So I have seen her more often lately than I had before. But even at this, it has only been several times.

And each time was sudden and unexpected. We would be in a closely heated discussion about this type of scalloping gear versus that type of scalloping gear, but for some reason I would look out from the crowd of us and there she would be sitting alone on a stool over there where the bar makes a corner. She would quietly meet my look, then she would smile that very personal smile. But then one of the others would say something that I simply had to dispute or else expand upon, and when I remembered her ten or fifteen minutes later and looked again, she would be gone. And each time it was as startling to see her gone, as it had been to first see her there.

That was when I was also trying to decide whether to get rigged to trawl for shrimp during the coming spring and summer. Every type of fishing requires special gear and special knowledge and different hours. So you go into new ventures only after much deliberation about whether it can pay and whether you will put in the hours so it will pay. Because you can work only so long a day whether day or night. And while you are doing one type of fishing you are not doing another type of fishing. So my decision about shrimping was important. And one evening we were giving it a thorough discussion and we stayed at the bar far later than usual and we had many more beers than usual. I left my crowd to go to the men's room, and as I was walking along behind the line of people on stools at the bar, there she was. I looked and she returned my look. But my trip to the men's room was quite urgent, so I was beyond her before she had a chance to smile. She was still there when I came back. When I stopped beside her she turned and looked up, then she smiled warm and easy and for only me. I said, "Look, I'm very attracted to you every time I see you. And I think you're very attracted to me also. I'm too dirty and tired and stinky and I've had too many beers for us to talk about it now. But I definitely think that we should talk about it sometime." She said, "I would like that," still smiling that smile. So I said, "All right," then I was back with my crowd.

But to tell the truth I simply forgot about that conversation. Because being a commercial fisherman is demanding and exhausting and time consuming. When you aren't gearing to fish, then you're fishing, and when you aren't fishing, then you're cleaning and repairing your gear so you can get geared again. And you must be repeatedly reminded of anything outside of that before it makes a real impact in this your closed life. So for a while I simply forgot about her, and her personal smile, and my wanting very much to make love to her. Then one evening last week here at the end of scallop season, we were again at the bar. For some reason again I looked, and again she was there, and again she smiled. But she was smiling at me in front of and beyond some guy who was sitting beside her and talking earnestly to her. And I could tell by her eyes that part of her smile was for only me. Then I could tell by her eyes that part of her smile that was for only him. And

117

suddenly I realized how much I had lost that I could have had. But it is just as well. Because my sea is a very jealous sea.

NINETEEN SEVENTY

Some of us survived the nineteen sixties better than other of us. Some perished. It was an equally wrenching decade for everyone all right. It was a necessary decade though. And it was a senseless decade also. And a great many were emotionally devastated by it for the rest of their lives. Particularly those who became so obsessed with one thing or another that they could not turn loose of that thing even when it had lost its need or had lost its support, or it had escalated into something far grander or far more ruthless. Because if you could not personally adjust quickly back then, then you would be crushed simply and swept aside rudely in our head long run away rush from crisis to trauma to crisis again. Because to say nineteen sixties is to say crisis and trauma indeed. And however much intact we still were when we survived them, just surviving them became something that we would have in common. Although very few since then have wanted to reminisce about the sixties as the good old days. And none since then have wanted to boast about the sixties as a decade that we could be proud of. It was like a huge war of confusion and madness on one vast sprawling battlefield with many separate armies fighting each other at the same time without beginning or end or let up or winner or loser. Just nonstop fighting and confusion and madness. Just one vast huge continuous war that rumbled and thundered and quaked back and forth and up and down to many separate banners that were constantly shifting and merging and splintering and redefining themselves only to emerge as many different banners. Nothing was sacred. Not anything and not anyone. And no family, no cause, no group, no community, no town, no city survived the sixties without their ranks of cripples and cowards and leaders and heroes. Much later it very likely will be considered a truly great decade by those who can only read about it. But to those of us who lived it, the best thing about the nineteen sixties was that it did end finally.

And for those of us who were fortunate enough to still be curious and to still be ambitious and to still have some innocence remaining when nineteen seventy began, was for us to then walk in the welcome warmth of a suddenly brighter day and a better day and a new day. Of course nothing had really changed at that exact moment except the numbers. And of course some of the loud craziness of the sixties continues even today as murmured rumbles somewhere within the sprawl. But when that taking forever clock did at last roll over the decade, an immediate and a long and a collective sigh of gigantic relief issued back and forth and up and down. And it was then okay for us all to stand down and go home. And so we did.

I know that Wes Hampton was glad when the sixties ended. Still, he did survive them much more intact than a lot of us. But that was because he somehow always knew when to turn loose of a thing before it carried him away with it to too far to return from intact. As things had done to so many of the devastated ones. So the riotous upheavals of all of us so hell bent on self destruction left only superficial scars on Wes. Not that he didn't care, because he did. Not that he wasn't involved, because he was. Because he did care deeply, and he was involved directly. But he had that special instinct of knowing when to turn loose while a thing was still personally positive, and before it became personally negative. And when you have that instinct then you never tire of caring or of becoming involved. Myself, I always had to be beaten furiously about the head and shoulders and have my death grip ripped away and be crushed simply and be swept tumbling aside rudely before I would turn loose. And this didn't have to happen very many times before soon I didn't care quite as much and soon I wasn't getting quite as involved. It was a special instinct that Wes had that not many of the rest of us had. And when he turned twenty eight during the summer of nineteen seventy, he was as curious and as ambitious and as innocent as ever. The rest of us turned twenty eight during that year also. And for us, twenty eight was to be the best age of any of them. We had stood down finally. We had gone home finally. And we were still single and we were responsible only to our work and to ourselves. We had begun to succeed quickly now, and with strides rather than steps, and we had acquired the maturity to realize this and to enjoy it thoroughly. We had the clothes and the cars and the looks and the experience and the sophistication, and plenty of the dynamic years still in front of us. Life had become simple for us at twenty eight back in nineteen seventy. Life had become easy for us at twenty eight back in nineteen seventy. Suddenly it was a brighter day and a better day and a new day. Yeah, and for us twenty eight would always be the best age of any of them.

Mickey had just turned twenty three when she and Wes first met at one of our reunion parties early in nineteen seventy. And

121

twenty three is the best age of any of them for young ladies who have begun their careers. Because it is for them what twenty eight was for us. But we were surprised at how quickly Wes and Mickey were attracted to each other. Because he was so out going and she was so quiet. And because their work was in opposites. But we were glad also. Because they did make a good looking couple standing there off to themselves so absorbed with only each other. But with Mickey living in Richmond, and with Wes having recently moved from High Point to his hometown near Morehead City, that distance plus their each being so busy pretty much kept them apart for most of that spring and summer. They were together in a crowd several other times with the rest of us up here. But it wasn't until that fall that Wes did actually start the twice before postponed trip to Richmond for their perfect weekend alone together at last. He really was excited as he put his suitcase in his car and started. She really was excited as she finished dressing and left for work. We certainly felt their excitement up here where we were in Raleigh and Greensboro and Charlotte. And we really were glad for them. And we were excited also as we left for our work that Friday morning.

The plum tree in the backyard where Wes lives is the first tree around there to wear full fall proudly. And on this Friday morning, with the everywhere frost that is in the chilled dew, it is startling in its display of burnt reds and fire golds. Of course in Richmond, just as up here, full fall had arrived also with its beautiful hold that is as hard and fast as it is fleeting. Because bleak winter surely follows. But during this weekend when Wes and Mickey walk

122

arm in arm along the worn brick streets to the downtown park, to sit alone together at last on an October dusty bench, they will wear fall's startling blanket snugly as though it has been woven for only them. And maybe it had. It's nice to think that it had. Because there is always one quick weekend when the days have shortened and the sunlight isn't as direct, so the leaves are well into their proud death, when we realize suddenly that final fall is very near. And too soon true cold will come to shrink and to shiver all the burnt leaves of fire. Too soon tearing wind will come to howl gusty winter that will naked all the trees, and fling their ten billion leaves to rattle and to scurry toward nowhere to hide. One weekend of beauty to remember until far spring.

We knew that Wes would get to Richmond in early afternoon. There is a nice downtown motel that is close to Mickey's apartment. He will check into a third floor room with a good view of the brick streets and the old shops and the many trees of the park. Then he will casually walk this good view. Because whenever possible men of twenty eight should be seen smartly dressed and confidently walking among the busy people and the busy shops of a downtown on a Friday afternoon.And to heighten the intrigue of who he is and why he is there when so many are hidden somewhere in offices and warehouses and factories, Wes will let several stunning women pass without even an appraising glance. But when a particularly dowdy specimen passes he will stop now stunned, then turn and quickly begin to follow her trudge as though he is absolutely astonished by such a welcome treasure find. Then the busy people will know that he certainly must be some master artist who is renowned and world traveling in disguise in a long vein search for that rarest of models with the faintest of silver smiles and the inner preciousness of the genuine. That finally he has found her, alas!, and among their own on their worn streets. But then only to frantically lose her in an every which way going crowd at the pedestrian intersection of a fate fickle stoplight. As back into obscurity goes this rare precious model, flabby arms loaded and numbed by too full shopping bags, ankles swollen and weary from the fatigue of her trudge. Then the shocked people will again cringe in the bitter sweet sadness that is always and ever in boy finds girl and boy loses girl. But Wes will only return to his motel room to casually read the thick columns of the tradings and the dealings and the merchandising's that are in the Wall Street Journal. Because whenever possible men of twenty eight should be as complex as they are mysterious.

Mickey will get to her apartment from work about six. When Wes phones she will say that she is so happy that he is here. Then she will ask when he arrived. And he will say not long ago. Because young ladies simply do not understand what men of twenty eight must do wherever possible on a Friday afternoon. Again she will say how happy she is that he is here. That he should hurry over right now. And he will.

Wes knew that this is how their perfect weekend would begin once he got to Richmond. At a service station before the freeway on ramp the attendant said, "thank you Mr. Hampton, stop again," when he returned the credit card to Wes. Being called Mr. Hampton still surprised Wes, as though it was his father who was being addressed. But it was nice to look more like a man now, after so long looking like a boy. But he missed the casual familiarity that is in first names too. At work in the furniture industry, as he had quickly advanced from foreman to supervisor to manager with several different companies, the employees had called him Wes just because he looked too young to be called Mr. Hampton. But recently he had begun to acquire a maturing around his eyes and along his chin that in time would become even more distinguished. Because to be twenty eight is to have gone through many changes. First the changes that are in going from the small world of your hometown to the larger world of college to the much larger world of work. Now the more subtle changes that come about while maturing. And as things are gained, thing are lost, and what you are and what you will become are a gradual reshaping of what you have been. But Wes wasn't certain that he was ready for the great change that he now found himself well into. Because on the spur of a moment he had started his own one man furniture manufacturing company. And this was proving to be the largest change so far, even though it had begun innocently enough.

Because in nineteen seventy we still believed that simple solutions could solve complex problems. And Wes as much so as any of the rest of us. And free enterprise was his favorite banner through which to do this. At a party just before he and Mickey met, there were others there who had their favorite banners also. Well sure enough, all this banner waving sparked rather heated debate that night, but this time with Wes as its focus. Because back then no one could discuss anything, whether politics or religion or economics, calmly and intelligently and reasonably. And every discussion fast became loud debates that faster still fell apart into full blown arguments that no one could possibly win. And this is what happened that night. Because we hadn't as yet all stood down and gone home, not completely. So with Wes as the focus of this argument, the others weren't winning as much as they had him far outnumbered and were out shouting him. The others certainly didn't agree among themselves, not by any means, except that free enterprise couldn't solve anything. That it long had been tried, that it had failed. That it was old fashion, and that it was time for new solutions. Well, Wes quickly became defensive of course, and was on the verge of becoming mad, being out shouted and outnumbered so. The rest of us fully expected him to just turn loose, before he became crushed simply and swept aside rudely. But suddenly he slammed his fist hard on a table and shouted, "all right! I'll show you all." And this is how the Hampton Chair Company got its one man start.

But we still expected Wes to turn loose once the loud heat of the argument had cooled. But that Monday he upped and gave notice at work. It was soon after that that he moved from High Point to his hometown near Morehead City. He leased a run down building on the waterfront that had been an ice house that supplied fishing boats. He bought some old wood working machines that the State Prison's were auctioning off. In the South Carolina low country he located a source of hardwoods. In Piedmont North Carolina he located sources of upholstery fabric and springs and padding. And then he began to build chairs. But not just any chair, not our Wes, rather great massive hand carved handmade lushly upholstered kings chairs. He took the slogan 'Chairs Fit For A King'. And they were splendid chairs indeed. Of course Wes had always been good at working with wood. And he had been in the industry long enough to learn the business fairly well. Still, you don't just go out and start a manufacturing company on the spur of a moment. One man, or not. At twenty eight, or any other age. This year, or any other year. And especially not in nineteen seventy. True, the me generation was in full stride back then. But those people had dropped out and turned on in a youthful fancy of self indulgence much as the lost generation had done back in the twenties. Because every generation has that segment. Just as every generation has its responsible segment. And Wes and the rest of us were pretty responsible. Because the impact of the great depression of the thirties on our parents had been carefully passed along to us. We had gone to college because that was expected of us. Then we had taken good jobs and had stayed with those jobs because that too was expected of us. Responsible people in nineteen seventy did not take risks. We just did not. Because security was very important to us. And we planned for the future. And we certainly did not make important decisions on the spur of a moment. But it was a time of isms also. Capitalism, communism, socialism, racism, welfareism, Republicanism, and on and on. There was an ism for all the philosophies. And every ism had its clear definition. And everyone was labeled according to their philosophy. And once labeled you could not deviate, much less change, from your ism. That became who you were, and what you were, and would always be so. And even to deviate would have meant a loss of credibility. And credibility was also very important to us back in nineteen seventy. So Wes having accepted capitalism as his philosophy, guess he felt that present credibility far out weighted future security. That was why he started the Hampton Chair Company on the spur of a moment. Because we were loyal to our isms. So now started, and with more hard work, and quality products at a fair price, profits would be generated. With these profits Wes would hire employees, increase production, then hire more employees, then increase production again. In time he would expand into other industries, always with quality products at a fair price, always in a steady progression of hiring employees and increasing production, to infinity. Which would improve the economic base of the town, the county, the State, the Nation, through greater personal income, through increased tax revenues, through the creation of related goods and services. Which in turn would reduce unemployment, reduce welfare, reduce government, reduce the national debt, and on and on. The clear capitalistic definition. But as I said, things were a lot simpler back in nineteen seventy.

But I'm sure that Wes didn't think that things were simple as he neared Richmond and Mickey that Friday. In fact the rest of us were concerned for Wes, as I'm sure he was concerned for himself. Because he had placed himself out on a very precarious limb back when just climbing a tree for the farther view that that provided wasn't really popular. But he never spoke his concern. And having started, he could only pursue this his one man adventure. Wes was the opposite of any man that Mickey had ever known. And she thought that what he was trying to do was both romantic and exciting. But I don't think she fully realized the responsibility involved or the probability of failure. Still they certainly were a good looking couple. Even their total absorption with each other whenever together was cute to the rest of us rather than rude. Mickey was continuing college at night in addition to her full time office job. And she was well into a one woman adventure to succeed on her own. She was a very attractive young lady. And neat. And tasteful too. Quite complete. Attractive and neat and tasteful. And you remembered her also for her smart choice in clothes. Because back then girls had stopped wearing dresses and were wearing jeans everywhere. Work, play, socially. So telling the girls from the boys had become more difficult. So Mickey's difference in clothes was quickly noticed. During the warm months she wore a variety of well coordinated linen skirts and cotton blouses both of pleasing pastels, with the blouses a shade lighter than the skirts and neck scarf's that matched. During the cold months she wore a second variety of well coordinated wool skirts and cashmere sweaters and matching neck scarf's that spanned the range of the charcoal browns and blues and blacks with complimentary yellows and pinks and lavenders. Years later this would be called the preppy look, and it would evolve into a formalized style of its own. But back in nineteen seventy it was just very refreshing to see a girl who dressed like a girl. And since Wes had stayed with traditional slacks rather than fad jeans, and button-down collar shirts and sports coats, they stood out together and were noticed wherever they went.

And as they stood just inside her apartment, her dark hair was longer than he remembered. And her perfume was more dizzying than he remembered. And their breathing quickened as their soft kiss continued. So he pressed her hard to him.

"Wait Wes." She turned her mouth from the kiss and rested her forehead on his shoulder. "I can't breathe."

"Mickey." Quick breathing the dizzying perfume of her long hair.

"It's too soon."

"I haven't seen you in two months."

"You just got here."

"I can't keep my hands off you."

"We have all weekend."

"Kiss me again."

"My heart will stop." Then she began walking from the foyer to the living room. "Come tell me how you've been." She was holding his hand and leading him toward the couch.

"Right now?" Him having only begun to settle down.

"Tell me about your chairs. I can't wait to hear about your chairs." Sitting with one leg crooked on the couch to face him sitting there beside her.

"Well, I've sold three so far. And I received orders for three more last week." Him almost settled down now.

"Oh Wes, that's wonderful."

"A good start. And I'll have several at the furniture show in Columbia next month."

"Isn't it exciting?!"

"It's scary."

"But exciting too. It is. And I'm so proud of you!"

"Exciting to you up here. But scary to me down there."

"You'll do it. I know you will. But shouldn't you have stayed in High Point?"

"The lease would have been expensive. And when I start hiring, the labor costs a lot more."

"Oh I'm so proud of you. I really am." Still holding his hand, and squeezing it again and again in her pride of him. And smiling her pride of him also. And he knew now that he did love her. And he knew that he would not be able to keep his hands off her.

"But I miss the gang, and I miss the parties. But it's nice to be back home too."

"When can I come down?"

"Whenever you want."

"I can't wait to see your chairs. Oh Wes!"

"They're special all right. People are stunned when the see them. But the price is still too high. Next is getting it down."

"You'll do it. I know you will." Still smiling her full pride of him. And he knew that he soon would tell her that he loved her. And that having said it to her this first time, he would never be able to stop saying it to her.

"You're so pretty, Mickey." And she was prettier than he remembered.

They ate in a very nice restaurant near her apartment. On each of their plates was a slab of medium rare roast beef that had just been thick sliced from a stand of roast beef as it stood deliciously smoking and still cooking in the buffet line. A ladle of the thin juices had been sluiced across these hot slabs. And a fluffy biscuit was big on the side of each plate. In small bowls were whole new potatoes boiled and now in butter. In other small bowls were early green peas fancy and now in butter also. And in third small bowls were ripe red tomato wedges with mayonnaise and salt and pepper. And when they did speak there in the seclusion of their out of the way table, it was hushed and private and tender. Because their perfect weekend had begun. And they were alone together finally.

Then they walked backed to her apartment along the night streets of the quiet downtown. Gone was the loud swarm of the day. For blocks ahead the solitary stoplights went from green to yellow to red, then to green again. But now without anyone to obey. They turned at a corner and began to walk the campus where Mickey took her courses. But this campus would never know the laughing splendor of a Saturday afternoon football crowd. Because this block of solemn buildings had been erected rather than constructed. And they were bunched without lawn or trees or flowers. Only a sidewalk grid of sharp angles was in between. Precast concrete subfloors had been placed within the tall steel frames. Then prefabricated modular rooms had been inserted before the glass panels and the precast facade had been applied. So there was neither the warmth of a college or the bustle of a trade school here. Because this was a modern institute that filled the needs of a changed society. And this was where specialized groups with singular interests took exact courses that had controlled objectives. So there was neither dormitory or gym or student union or library here. And the light that reflected from the glass panels of the bunched buildings was a sterile light. And the people who hurried among these erected buildings were grim with the heavy problems of the poor.

But Mickey was proud of this campus as they walked hand in hand through it and she talked about her courses. And she wanted Wes to be as proud of her as she was of him. Because she had been selected from sixty three other social workers to take this one year advanced curriculum in welfare administration. And in her classes were the eleven other winners of their respective regions. So this was a select group indeed. Because they would be the future administrators in this highly specialized new field. In her courses they analyzed previous welfare cases in order to begin to better understand the proper dispersal of public monies to the poor. And in these courses they sought the economic and the social and the historic reasons that caused the poor. And they recommended various motivations that might rehabilitate the poor. And they discussed great plans of preventive measures that might break the cycle of the poor. And in these courses they made long lists of additional urban factor and industrial factors and rural factors that detrimentally effected and affected the poor. Because in nineteen seventy man believed that a blank check from the federal government could solve any problem.

But what Mickey said as they walked through the campus startled Wes. Because everyone worked in the towns where he had lived. Of course some had better jobs than others. And some of the jobs were menial and at the minimum wage. But everyone worked at some job. And the family took care of those who couldn't work. So there simply were not able people around who were not working. So paying people to not work was a foreign concept in these towns. So it did truly startle Wes to now hear that in the cities a war had been declared on poverty and that the welfare of the poor had become a fulltime occupation for large groups of others. That the poor now were the single focus of a complex curriculum at a modern institute. That they alone had become an exact career for these highly trained professionals. But along with being startled Wes was also disturbed that Mickey had so intense of an unfamiliar world that was so apart from him and his world. The ice cubes were small and the scotch was pale. And their cigarettes were burned grey lines in the ashtray as they lay in each others arms on the couch and kissed short kisses and spoke closely.

"Don't be mad."

"I'm not."

"You are."

"No I'm not."

"I had to stop."

"It's okay."

"I wasn't going to stop."

"We have all weekend."

"Our weekend."

"Our perfect weekend."

"I've thought about it so often."

"So have I."

"But I wasn't going to stop."

"It's okay."

 "Don't be mad."

"I'm not."

"Be patient."

"I will. "

"It's different with girls."

"I know. Well, I think I know. But beyond a point boys just can't stop."

"I know. Well, I think I know."

"It's complicated."

"But I wasn't going to stop. I've dreamed about it. But in the dreams I didn't stop."

"Girls aren't supposed to dream about it. Boys dream about. But girls don't."

"Sure we do. At least I have been with you."

"What did you dream?"

"I can't tell you."

"Tell me."

"I can't. We were naughty."

"Tell me."

"I can't. We were terrible. We were naughty."

"Good. Let's be naughty again."

"We were. Oh look, now I'm blushing."

"You are!"

"Don't look."

"You're beautiful when you blush."

"No I'm not."

"Yes you are, and I want you."

"And I want you too."

"Then don't stop."

"I don't plan to. Then something makes me."

"Don't listen to it." "I tell myself not to. Then I do." "Only think about the kiss. This kiss."

"- - -Wes - - - Wes- --Wes!" "What?"

"Wait.

"Why?"

"- - - Wes!"

"What?"

"Wait."

"Ah hell."

"Don't be mad."

"I'm not."

"You are."

"Dammit I'm not."

"- - - Wes - - - Wes!"

"Okay! I'll wait."

"I've always stopped. So not stopping now isn't easy."

"We have all weekend."

"And it will happen when it happens."

"Now?"

"No, not now silly."

"When?"

"Soon."

"How soon?"

"Just soon."

"Tomorrow?"

"Maybe tomorrow."

"Promise?"

"I promise - - - maybe.

" Because in nineteen seventy there were young ladies who did use the word naughty, and who were still virgins at twenty three.

The rest of us here had begun to gather on that Saturday morning for another of our regular parties. But of course this one would be without Wes and Mickey. So we were anxious to know how their weekend together finally was going. And we wished for an unseen observer there with them in Richmond who could tell us how they were getting along. Not that we wanted to know the personal that happened between them, because that really was their business only. Rather because Mickey was easy to like and fun to be with, and because she was the first girl in a long while who we felt would be good for Wes. Because without actually being aware of it, the rest of us had begun to look somewhat beyond this magical age of twenty eight and the temporary plateau of youth with sophistication and excitement with security that it represented, and gradually had begun to comfortably settle in with the one girl who for whatever reasons had chosen the each of us.

And because Wes had never been very open about what went on between he and whichever girl he was with at the time. So we knew that we would not hear from him how things went with Mickey. Before, as long as we saw Wes together with a girl we knew that they were getting along. Then when we no longer saw them together we knew that they had stopped getting along. But then it took a little extra determination from the girl to get along with Wes. Not that he was overly demanding or terribly difficult, because he wasn't. Rather because there was a single mindedness about Wes that none of the rest of us had to quite that extent. And if a girl could not accept this in him, and none had been able to so far, then sure enough it wouldn't be long before they stopped getting along. Because in his single mindedness Wes was a bore, but without really being boring. This isn't my description of him, rather the description of a particularly astute girl who he was with for awhile a year or so ago. She said that Wes was very much aware of life, and probably more aware of life than most people, but that he could focus his attention on only a few things in life at a time. And that this focus was so intense and so restricted on these few things that there simply wasn't room for other things. And that was why she said Wes was a bore, but without really being boring. Of course the rest of us had known him since our freshmen year in college and we had long accepted him the way he was, so we had to think about her description for awhile before we could agree. And even though we did come to agree with her, we did not try to change Wes. So we could only hope that a girl would come along who could accept him the way he was the way that we accepted him the way he was. And in Mickey we thought we saw that special girl. Because she certainly seemed to have chosen Wes from the first moment they were together. And she did not seem to want to be apart from him even briefly. And she seemed to hang on his every word the way that girls do when they really have decided. And we thought that their attraction for each other was because they were so similar in so many ways. Both bright and alert and good looking. Both very involved and hard working. But quite soon we saw that Mickey had a single mindedness about herself also. At least she did when it came to her social work. Not that she talked about it that often, because she didn't, and in fact she seldom talked about it. But the few times when she did talk about it, there was an intensity toward it and a restricted focus about it that startled us. Of course we were use to this in Wes, but in Mickey it was truly surprising. Because before now girls just did not commit themselves to things to quite that extent. So while this similarity was much of their early attraction, we came to fear that it might also become responsible for their eventual repulsion. Because this was at a time when sudden upheavals and dramatic conflicts and sharp divisions among people were frequent and usual and strong. Because the stark difference between the past and the future, the tried and the untried, were painfully clear indeed to all of us back then. And it certainly wasn't uncommon for friends and families and communities and cities to be racked and ravaged and then split forever over a single basic simple issue. So we hoped that Wes and Mickey were getting along well together on this their perfect weekend alone together finally. And we hoped that they, too, would not get terribly caught up in these very very emotional times. And divided forever as so many of us had become divided forever.

Full fall had arrived that Saturday afternoon there in the park with its beautiful hold that is as hard and fast as it is fleeting. Because bleak winter surely follows. And when they sat alone together on the October dusty bench they wore falls' startling blanket snugly as though it had been woven for only them. And maybe it had. It's nice to think that it had.

Because there is always one quick weekend when the days have shortened and the sunlight isn't as direct, so the leaves are well into their proud death, when we realize suddenly that final fall is very near indeed. And too soon true cold will come to shrink and to shrivel all the burnt leaves of fire. Too soon tearing wind will come to howl gusty winter that will naked all the trees, and fling their ten billion leaves to rattle and to scurry toward nowhere to hide. One weekend of beauty to remember until far spring.

Then they stood on the ridge with falls' pale sky beyond them. Such a good looking young couple. Her in a charcoal grey skirt and matched set of pink pullover sweater then button front sweater and a grey flowered neck scarf. Him in brown slacks and white open collared shirt and tan sports coat. Her hair already the dark of winter. His hair still the fair streaked of summer. And Wes showed Mickey the directions with specific finger points that led to large areas sweeps of his arm. "Our defense began there where the downtown now begins. We were pushed back to this ridge, then later to that ridge behind us there before we counter attacked. But our counter attack stalled at this ridge. Then the fighting settled down and became sporadic as it flared then quieted and shifted along this ridge eastward, around to there, then more south of downtown way over there. Finally after a week of mostly stalemate, we loaded into boats and went down the James River there. But during that week of fighting the people came and stood on the hills and the buildings of the then downtown there and watched each day's battles as though they were panoramic movies for only them. The Yankees could see them clearly there on the sidelines too. Then on an especially critical day toward the end of the week, a terrible thunderstorm moved over the Yankee positions that were along that ridge there. And while the rain pounded and drenched them, and the lightning flashed and crashed all about them, a perfect rainbow that was towering and brilliant formed above us here with its ends coming down at the outer limits of our line there and there. And then everyone knew that the rainbow over us foretold the success of this defense of Richmond."

"You weren't here."

"My great grandfather was here. So I was here."

So Mickey looked at Wes with concern for a long moment. But he only continued to look across the now healed battlefield with the far away remembering well look that all old veterans have when they have returned.

"Wes, you were not here."

"Yes, I was here."

"Wes, you're frightening me."

So he quickly came back from where he had been. "No, Mickey, no." And he took her in his arms. "It just feels as though I were here."

"Please don't do that again." She said still concerned.

"No." But once again he was looking across the battlefield and remembering well.

"Wes."

"Yes."

"Let's go."

"In a minute."

"No, now, Wes."

So he looked at her and saw that she was still frightened.

"Alright."

Then they were walking hand in hand back through the October weekend park. Such an attractive couple. Certainly the future is theirs.

"What terrible waste."

"What tremendous glory."

"What's glorious about that much pain and death?"

"That both sides fought so valiantly."

"But we were wrong to start it."

"We fired the first shot. But we didn't start it."

"But slavery was wrong. We were wrong."

"Slavery was the excuse, not the reason. Economics was the reason."

"Oh come on, Wes, you don't really believe that?!"

"No war is fought until bankers and businessmen have a reason for that war to be fought. The North had grown and industrialized, while the South continued backward and agricultural. Trade had been handled through the North. But gradually we gained in ships and expertise until we could handle our own timber and furs and textiles and crops. Then we could trade with the world without the North as middlemen. War was the only way their bankers and businessmen could protect their interests."

"Wes, you don't seriously believe that?!"

"Think about it, Mickey. Slaves simply filled a need. Because working a thousand acres is more efficient than working a hundred acres. And working ten thousand acres is more efficient still. We had the land and the climate. But we didn't have the labor. So Northerners brought us the labor and sold it to us. Then we could produce more to sell to them so they could resell to the world. Slaves were good for business. The morality of slavery came much later."

"Wes, that's the most ridiculous thing I've ever heard!"

"Mickey, you're comparing the South now with the South of more than a hundred years ago. That's comparing apples with oranges. Richmond and Charlotte and Columbia and Atlanta and Birmingham and New Orleans were just large towns. A mile or so from the small towns was still an underdeveloped frontier. The few dirt roads quickly became trails. Our railroad system had only just begun. Newspapers were local only. The mail took weeks to be delivered. The people were independent and self sufficient, the kind it takes to carve and hold something from the wilderness. The plantations began in Virginia because it was close to the North, then around New Orleans because it was such a big shipping port. But the rest of the plantations were widely scattered in between. The majority of the people survived on what they could scratch from a hundred acres. Their closest neighbor might be five miles away, and they only saw them several times a year. There was little cash, so they bartered. Their ten or fifteen kids were their labor source. But they could identify with the few who had acquired enough so they could own slaves. They could identify with their neighbor and their town and their State. They couldn't identify with a Union that included people who were so far from them and so different from them. So when these outsiders began saying that none could own slaves, they quickly joined with their neighbors against the outsiders. But they didn't go to war to preserve slavery, they went to war because of the outside interference."

"Wes, that's the silliest reasoning I've ever heard.!"

"What do you mean?!"

"Just what I said!"

"Well, what I said is true to how it was, not how history has recorded it."

"Well, there weren't any plantations in the North Carolina mountains. And I rarely saw a black growing up in Asheville. But I've always known without being taught that slavery is wrong. That no human being has the right to own another human being. They simply don't. And if only one slave was owned in the South, and the rest of the South defended that, then the South was wrong and I'm glad we were defeated."

"Mickey, you're comparing the morals now with those of more than a hundred years ago, and again that's comparing apples with oranges.

"Oh shut up with the apples and oranges, Wes!"

"Mickey, you aren't being fair or realistic."

"Your fair and realistic is just making excuses. You can explain it anyway you want, and justify it anyway you want, but it still comes back to this one simple fact --- that no human being has the right to own another human being, now, then, ever. Not ever, not anywhere. And since you choose to defend them, then you are wrong. Terribly wrong, and I'm terribly upset at hearing you talk this way. I certainly expected more from you."

They were suddenly silent now as they continued to walk back through this October park. Something was different. Everything had changed. Both were stung now, and each had withdrawn into their separate rages. Suddenly they had become two apart. No longer were they two together. Because they, too, could be caught in the upheavals. Because they, too, could be split forever, as so many of us had become split forever in nineteen seventy. So this final fall day became merely the fittingly bleak background, while the scurrying leaves still had nowhere to hide.

But however much that had been stolen from it, however many shadows that had arisen around it, this was still their perfect weekend together finally. Each had expected so much that would come from it. Each had imagined so much that would come from it. Each had hoped that so much would come from it. So he did not pack his car and leave immediately. So she did not demand that he do so. They simply cringed quietly and alone, and waited, hope upon hope.

So he went to his motel room to change clothes, then to sit for awhile at the large window and watch evening come to the downtown park. So she went to her apartment to change clothes, then to begin preparations for the spaghetti supper. He would come at seven. The other couple would come at eight.

She answered the door before his ring had really faded. And even though something was different, and everything had changed, for a moment they were again in each others arms. Because there still was hope. Then she returned to the preparations in the small kitchen that was just off from the living room, while he made a drink then sat on the couch where he could see her moving about. Because there is always hope.

Mickey had only said that a couple from the college was coming over. But when they arrived, Wes was very surprised that Mickey was friendly with such people. They wore old army fatigue coats and faded shirts and worn jeans. Their shoulder length hair had not been combed, and they looked painfully thin and drained. Their eyes were itchy red and dark circled as though they were feverish. People such as these were seen more and more frequently these days, at the colleges and the airports and along the streets of the cities. But the seeing of them was always startling and never pleasant. After her first look and nod and hello, the girl neither looked at Wes or spoke to him for the rest of the evening. The guy gave Wes only fingers to shake, and they were soft and moist and quickly withdrawn. Then the guy asked if Wes was at the college. When Wes said no, that he manufactured chairs, the guy did not look at Wes or speak to him for the rest of the evening either. Mickey tried several times to include Wes in the conversations, but each time the couple completely ignored him. Finally he stopped even the half hearted attempts to join in. And as his dislike for the couple grew and became more apparent, Mickey first began to nervously pat his hand in her lap. Then she just desperately held his hand with both of her hands. Because Wes did not want such people anywhere around Mickey, and she knew it.

The couple was also in the one year advanced curriculum in welfare administration. For their next weeks assignment, they were writing a joint paper titled, The Psychological Effects Of Rats In The Homes Of Adolescent Children Of The Poor. Mickey's paper for that assignment was titled, The Effects Of Television On Teenage Pregnancy Among The Poor. The research and the statistics and the conclusions and the recommendations were the only conversations that evening.

Wes had never before been around people who were grim with the heavy problems of the poor. He had not realized that the poor needed new professionals to understand their behavior. He had not realized that the poor needed more assistance than a swift kick in the rear to get a job. Mickey often became intense when talking about her work and the college, but Wes attributed this to enthusiasm and to dedication and to youth. But the couple was obsessed by the poor to the righteous exclusion of all else. Because the pendulum that so long had been where the poor were totally ignored, now had swung to where the poor were the absolute

147

center of concern. So a war on poverty had been declared, with every resource marshaled, and the couple was at the frontline of the crusade. Because great dignity had at last come to those who could not work or would not work. But Wes did not want Mickey to have any part of any of this. But he dare not say it. Because having just come so very close to losing her, he wasn't about to jeopardize things again. So when they were alone and washing and drying and putting away the dishes, when Mickey repeatedly apologized for the couples rudeness saying that she didn't know they would act that way, all Wes said was "that's alright, it doesn't matter." And it truly didn't matter. Because only Mickey mattered. Because now he was going to tell her that he loved her. And saying it to her this first time, he knew that he would never be able to stop saying it to her.

"I love you, Mickey."

"Oh Wes, you said it."

"I love you, Mickey, I love you, I love you."

"Oh, and I love you. I do. Hold me close." So he held her close. And the perfume in her long dark hair was as dizzying as always.

"I still can't keep my hands off you."

"It's okay now, touch me. I won't stop us.'

"You won't?"

 "No."

"Why?"

"Because I almost lost you this afternoon, and I don't want to lose you."

"Whoa, Mickey, making love shouldn't be a price you pay."

"I know. But the more we share, the closer we are. Then we can't lose each other. Besides I've taken precautions."

"What precautions?"

"Just precautions."

"Which one?"

"You know."

"What did you do, Mickey?" Laughing.

"Don't laugh, I'll blush."

"You already are."

"I know. Don't look."

"You are truly beautiful, and I love you."

"And I won't stop us."

"Maybe you should."

"It's my decision."

"But I'm also responsible."

 "But I've taken precautions."

 "But I'm also responsible."

"Will I look different?"

"Maybe a little more experienced in the eyes."

 "Then it won't be in big letters across my forehead?"

"No, silly," laughing again, "no more than the virgin is there now."

"Maiden, Wes, please. I'm a maiden in waiting. But we won't wait any longer."

"I love you so, Mickey, and I can't keep my hands off you."

"Then don't. Touch me here."

"Mickey."

"What?"

"No."

"Why?"

"Just no."

The rest of us here had pretty well gotten out of hand at the party last night, as we tended to do with some regularity now, so we were feeling rather ragged as we packed our cars that Sunday afternoon and got ready to return to our own cities. Because once a girl has definitely picked you, for whatever her reasons, then you can become a bit more outrageous in your behavior without the fear of having to go out tomorrow and begin again to find a girl who will pick you. So while we were feeling ragged as we half heartedly packed our cars, the girls who we had more or less settled down with were alternating between scolding us and shaking their heads among themselves. And when you are twenty eight and quite dynamic and have so very much going for you, it is very nice to be mothered and fussed over also. But amid our raggedness and half hearted packing and scoldings, we stopped several times to wonder out loud how the perfect weekend had gone for Wes and Mickey and whether they had gotten along. We would find out soon, but for now all we could do was hope and be anxious. Because they certainly were such a good looking couple.

And as they stood beside his already packed car that Sunday afternoon, all bundled against the final fall Richmond wind, they held each other close.

"Can you come down home the weekend after next?"

"If you want me to."

"You know I do."

"Then say it."

"Mickey, I want you to come down home the weekend after next."

"Yes, Wes." She said as though she had just given herself completely to him.

"Mom wants to meet you, and you can see my chairs. And if it isn't too cold we'll take my skiff over to Shackleford Banks and walk on the beach."

"Yes, Wes." She said looking up at him with the softest eyes he had ever seen.

"And stop looking at me that way."

"Yes, Wes."

"The answer is still no. I like the thought of you as a maiden in waiting."

"Your maiden in waiting."

"Our maiden in waiting."

"Thank you, Wes. I love you, and I'm proud of you. But don't make we wait too long."

"It will be something fine that we have to enjoy and share."

"Don't get carried away with it, Wes."

"We'll know when the time is right."

"Maybe the weekend after next?"

"We'll see."

"Yes, Wes." But standing there among the scurrying October leaves, they simply could not keep their hands off each other.

"Mickey, I do love you so."

"Yes, Wes. Yes."

Wes and Mickey were married that next summer, after she had completed her one year course at the college. The rest of us, some with more reluctance than others, married also during that time. Myself, though, Pam finally had to beat me furiously about the head and shoulders and rip away my death grip and drag me kicking and screaming to the altar. But then it always was me to not turn loose of anything gracefully while my dignity was still intact.

Wes moved his chair manufacturing to High Point soon after he and Mickey were married. Because now that he was into full production, experienced workers were more important than inexpensive workers. And because being near the furniture shows, and therefore the store buyers, was more important than low rent. Soon after he introduced a 'Chair Fit For a Queen', to go with his Kings Chair. But his chairs remained specialty items that appealed to a small percentage of the market. So while he did make a very good living from them, they didn't make him rich. Mickey was in her glory with the number of poor that were around Greensboro and High Point and Winston Salem. So the people that Wes couldn't help with a job, Mickey helped with welfare. Because it was a new era indeed. And they continued to be as remarkable a couple as when they first met. But after the urgency of their love calmed a bit, their personal intensity and strong beliefs resumed. The rest of us feared that their loud and usual arguments would destroy their marriage. But always, after trading finger pointing shout for finger pointing shout, they simply turned loose of whatever it was that had started the argument. And always, they ended with holding each other close. Because they never could keep their hands off each other.

So some of us did survive the nineteen sixties better than others of us. Some perished. It was an equally wrenching decade for everyone all right. It was a necessary decade though. And it was a senseless decade also. And a great many were emotionally devastated by it for the rest of their lives. Because to say nineteen sixties is to say crisis and trauma indeed. And few since have wanted to reminisce about the sixties as the good old days. And much later it very likely will be considered a truly great decade by those who can only read about it. But to those of us who lived them, the best thing about the nineteen sixties was that they did end finally. And when that taking forever clock did at last rollover the decade, an immediate and a long and a collective sigh of gigantic relief issued back and forth and up and down. Because it then was nineteen seventy, and therefore okay for us all to stand down and to go home. And so we did.

THE WORSE SCRAPE THERE EVER WAS

There for awhile it was a real scrape, the worse scrape there ever was. A sure enough tight, a bind, and between a rock and a hard place too. But even those of us who are on saltwater everyday get into them, even though we are always mighty wary whenever we are out there where harm hides playfully. And they only take a heartbeat to get into, then a lifetime to get out of. One moment you're wave dancing along as pretty as you please, then the next moment you're edge dangling and only a whisper away from being crabbait. Yeah, scrapes do happen. And they're always a time, the worst time, always an "oh shit!" and a butt puckering time.

It happened one day when the Fox had just left the dock in his fast sports fishing boat to go work his line of sea bass pots. He got that nickname because he has always been far too calculating and crafty and conniving for his own good, and for anyone else's good for that matter. And he has always liked that name, even though the rest of us fishermen gave it to him because we did not like him. Not at all. Because the Fox will say anything or do anything for an easy dollar of someone else's money. And he is the only man that I have known who has never had at least one friend. Not a buddy, not even another person that he was friendly with. We always went this way or went that way, we always did this or did that, but there was the Fox always alone though always among us, like a small stationary island in the middle of a big moving river. But it never seemed to bother him, in fact, he never seemed to even be aware of his isolation. He was happy with things the way they were, and the Fox would always be the Fox, so you could either take that or leave it, so we always just left it. Why, one time he even went so far as to take out a life insurance policy on his damn near dead from vodka brother. That really tore it with us here along the waterfront. But he was actually proud of his foresight, and he still is boasting about his forthcoming windfall and how he's going to spend it, since the sad event hasn't yet happened but still can anyway now. Because even though vodka is a slow killer, it is sure enough a sure killer finally. Yeah, the Fox is definitely an asshole. But his sports fisherman will flat fly, that it will, with the hundred and fifty horse throwing a one story rooster tail all the way and he works a damn good line of pots. And he makes good money from sea bass while none of the rest of us can. So we have to give him that, even though it irks the pure hell out of us to do so.

So the Fox had Rascal at about half throttle, and he had just begun to think about bringing her up to plane now that the dock was far enough behind. Her bow was raised sassily and her stern was lowered down deep and shoving powerful seas for a wake. He was well into the slow turn before the long straight that runs past the waterfront here, that slow turns again before going on to the ocean inlet. And he was rared back standing there at Rascal's center console, and struttingly filled with himself as usual, and it was at the end of the first slow turn that he showered down on

Rascal full throttle as though he planned on being his own one man one boat parade for any and for all who might be watching.

Well sir, the steering wheel was the car type, a round plastic rim with three aluminum spokes inside. And when Rascal's leaping forward thrust from full throttle hit the Fox, he quite naturally gripped real tight on the plastic rim to keep from being thrown back and away from the console. But the aluminum spokes somehow failed, because just in that heartbeat there was the still gripped real tight wheel pulled loose in his hands and coming up fast, and down there on the dashboard was the screw and clampdown nut where the wheel should have been. And just that suddenly "oh shit!" time was here, as his butt string had already begun to draw itself into a hard knot pucker. Because in the next heartbeat the Fox was thrown quickly aft and to starboard from the thrust, with the now turned loose wheel flying high overhead and dead astern over the hundred and fifty horse and sinking as it hit the water. But the sunk wheel only beat the Fox to the water by a half of the third heartbeat though. But the Fox was flailing wildly and panic grabbing for anything solid while on this sudden journey overboard and somehow managed to get his left arm hooked into a gunnel storage pocket. So there he was, from the waist up hanging onto Rascal's side for dear life, and from the waist down being dragged through the water like a ragdoll man. With Rascal having immediately set herself into full throttle teardrop shaped ovals that were wide on one end and closed on the other end, and eccentrically looping themselves along the waterfront. Yep, the Fox was in a sure enough scrape now, the worse scrape there ever was. And he certainly was a one man- one boat parade there for awhile, although not quite the proud parade that he had planned. And me and Larry just happened to be coming out of the Sea Squire after breakfast and heading for the dock. And we both looked across at about the same time and saw Rascal taking the Fox for the ride of his life. Before either of us could say "what the hell!", we both knew what the hell, so we lit out on a run to the dock to get a skiff that could catch Rascal.

By the time Larry had the outboard started and revving, I had the skiff untied and shoved off. Then we were out and coming up to run along side Rascal like the good cowboys having caught the runaway stage. Except the Fox sure as hell wasn't a pretty blond damsel in distress. Because pure terror was so deeply imprinted on his face that I didn't think that it would ever relax. And I could see his mouth moving as he talked to himself, but I couldn't hear what he was saying because of the two side by side screaming outboards. But I was certain that he had already so fouled the water around here that the Fisheries man would close all shellfishing for a week. And I also thought that if this had to happen to anyone, it couldn't have happened to a more deserving fellow. Then I yelled "turn loose!" to him when we were running close along side Rascal. But the Fox shook his head "no". So I yelled "turn loose!" again, but again he shook his head "no". So I picked up the skiffs poling oar and held it over my head like axe about to be chopped, and yelled "turn loose, or I'll goddamn knock you loose!" But the Fox yelled back "pants", then yelled "prop!" So I looked down at his in the water and being dragged half and saw that he was completely naked there. That the water force had turned his pants inside out as it had stripped them and his shorts down to his shoes, and that the trailing pants were fluttering under the water only a foot or so from the pounding prop of the hundred and fifty horse. So the Fox couldn't climb back in Rascal because of the drag of his pants. And he was afraid to turn loose because his pants might get caught in the prop, which would have surely wound the Fox up like a rubberband and bad hurt him forever in the process. Yep, the Fox was in a hell of a mess all right. A real between a rock and a hard place mess. But we had to get him away from Rascal. Then we had to get Rascal stopped and the one had to come before the other. So I dropped the about to be chopped poling oar and yelled "she'll slide away in this next closed turn, pull up your knees and push away then". And in that closed turn, she did, so he did, then Rascal was starting into the wide part of that oval and the Fox was bobbing and spitting there in the water. I had him up and into the bottom of the skiff before Rascal had even started back. Then Larry gunned the outboard and had us safely out of Rascal's runaway range.

While the Fox was sitting drenched in the bottom of the skiff getting his soggy shoes off so he could get his soaking wet pants and shorts off, then right side out and put back on, he kept muttering to himself "Jesus Christ!" and "Bloody Jesus!" and "Jesus H. Christ!" in every possible combination. And as I stood there watching him, I tried very hard to feel the normal great relief and the heightened affection that usually happens when a friend is dramatically removed from real harm finally, but all this seemed quite impersonal to me, and just another rescue, like firemen and policemen and Coast Guard men perform routinely, an all in days work sort of a thing. But the terror had suddenly relaxed from his face and that surprised me. But in its place his face had become very tired and very sagged and he looked as though he had aged ten years there before my eyes and that surprised me also. Because only five minutes had passed since this scrape had started.

Then the Fox had his soaking wet pants and shorts back on right side out. But he left his soggy shoes to lie where they were. The muttered Jesus Christ combinations having stopped. The pure terror imprint having relaxed, and suddenly now the aged ten years look replaced itself with a very flushed look. Then in a gush he began to tell about the pants and the prop thing and about being afraid to turn loose, and about being unable to climb back aboard, then about being afraid that if he had gotten clear without getting wound up bad that Rascal might well have run him over on her next oval. And the more he told about all that, the faster he talked and the more excited he became. Now his face was really flushed and his eyes were wide and wild, and still getting wider and wilder. So I yelled "hey!" at him and I told him to shut the hell up real loud. That we could bullshit about all that later. Then his face went totally blank just that quickly as though I had hit him there with a wet fish. But with Rascal's eccentric ovals, she now had worked her way to too close to the one after the other private docks that were along the waterfront there.

Where a bunch of fine pleasure boats were tied off and idling waiting like so many sitting ducks for the runaway destruction that Rascal was. So the Fox wasn't the problem now, because Rascal was the problem now. So Larry asked him how much gas she had and he said that he had just topped off both tanks. So she certainly wouldn't stop on her own anytime soon. So I said "run ahead of her and I'll throw a line for her to run over and that'll wind in her prop and she'll stop." But the Fox said "yeah, then I'll have to spend three hundred dollars for a new prop." So Larry said, "okay, then I'll put our stern alongside her bow and use our wake to turn her toward that bank there." He pointed to where and said "she'll ground and that'll kill the motor," and that sounded like a good idea to me. But right away the Fox said "no, she'll stove her bottom running aground." Some of the excited look had returned to his face after the totally blank look had faded, but not much of the flushed look though. So I said, "the stoving can be fixed, but we damn well better get her stopped soon because she's about to do a million dollars worth of damage to those boats there." Then I pointed but the Fox just shook his head no. Then he said "run close alongside, Larry, I'll jump aboard and kill the switch." But Larry said "that's plain crazy, Fox, she'll swamp us that close, or you'll fall short or fall on something and get hurt." But the Fox said "do it Larry, I can make it, but I can't let her get stoved," and all this was said in only a minute or so. So Larry looked at me and I looked at him, Then I shrugged as if to say, give it a try, it's his boat and his ass .

So then we were out and running fast with runaway Rascal once again. And Larry got us positioned inside of her ovals and we made several of these with her, so Larry and the Fox could gauge her speed and distance and turning. And when Larry felt good about these, he ran us right up alongside during the wide part of that oval. But Rascal's powerful wake got us and, with our skiff being much lighter, shoved us off and aft. And by now the private docks and the fine pleasure boats were really close so I figured that all hell was just about to break loose with a lot of shit hitting a very big fan. So on the next wide part, Larry ran a little ahead of Rascal so she would catch up to us, but when she did we banged hard together and that threw the Fox's balance off enough so he didn't jump. So Larry said, "I'll do that again, jump right before the bang." And the Fox nodded okay and his face looked really excited again. I just stood there in the skiff looking from Larry to the Fox and back to Larry then back to the Fox and felt useless without anything to do. So Larry did, then the Fox did, then me and Larry were quickly away from Rascal after that bang, while the Fox was in midair, then was spilled on her floor boards, then was crashing about inside of her out of our sight. But then the Fox was up and scrambling like a wildman, and when he killed the switch the screaming hundred and fifty horse died immediately. Rascal settled down playfully and just sat there rocking and rolling in her own wake.

So it was over. It really was over! It finally was over. But ten minutes hadn't yet passed. So me and Larry looked at each other and we shook our head in amazement, then we both said "wwhheewww!" together. Because it really was over. But it had been a real tight for sure there for awhile. And they only take a heartbeat to get into, then a lifetime to get out of. But the only damage was that the Fox had been on the ride of his life with his pride taking a pretty good thumping in the process. Because watermen, especially, ain't supposed to get thrown from their boats. We just ain't. But the Fox came through it still the conniving Fox. And we could still take that or leave it. And we still chose to leave it. But you would think that an experience like this would change a man for the better. But not the Fox. Because he continued to spend the insurance policy money before he got it. And even said that he was going to double the payoff since there wasn't any way that his brother could live much longer. Yep, the Fox is definitely an asshole. But there for awhile it was a scrape, the worse scrape there ever was.

FREE MEN

The word is that the Pamplico Sound behind Portsmouth Island is blowed full of clams at twenty feet of water. But you would have to be a commercial clammer to understand how this truly fires our imaginations, and makes us want to be gone there now for a dawn launching of our skiffs. And you would have to be a commercial clammer to realize what the possibility of a pot of gold at the end of the rainbow such as this would mean to us. Because we scour and we scrounge day after day to grind out our five to seven hundred clams. And it is heartbreaking, and it is hard, and it is monotonous. But when you say that a place is blowed full of clams, you are talking about a carpet of clams a foot deep in the bottom for miles. Just waiting there for us to come and get them, to harvest them, to reap them, to be awash in clams, finally. Because clams are money, and money is to us what it is to everyone else. But we are already free men on a little money. But a lot of money would mean complete freedom for however long or short that the lot of money might last. Then it would be back to just being free men on a little money. But think of the fine memories that we would have, think of the grand sea stories that we could tell as old men, of this our one great and glorious bonanza. So the word all along the bar at the Jolly Roger right now is that the Pamplico Sound is blowed full of clams. You're talking about six to eight thousand clams a day, just for the going out there and the taking of them. But at twenty feet of water, and the only way that a commercial clammer could reach this depth would be with a bullrake with a sixty foot handle. And working sixty feet of handle is not easy, and it is not simple, no not at all. And with a twenty mile an hour southwest wind, the Pamplico Sound gets rougher than the Atlantic Ocean does with a fifty mile an hour northeast wind. The Pamplico Sound is a widow maker, that is for sure. We can be in a real scrape out there and become sudden history, all in the first instant that it takes for us to recognize that we're in a real scrape. The Pamplico Sound does not care that we bend and we break and we bleed out there upon her alone and tiny in our puny skiffs. She is truly cold, she is, and she just does not care. But the patent tong boats can beat her mechanically, and bulk get all her clams laughing. But now you're talking corporations, you're no longer talking commercial clammers. Patent tong boats ain't free. Corporations ain't free. The Pamplico Sound is free. Commercial clammers are free. So the word is that the Pamplico Sound behind Portsmouth Island is blowed full of clams at twenty feet of water for miles. And just the thinking about all them out there just waiting drives us pure crazy to be gone there now for a dawn launching of our skiffs.

I DIED

I died. But it was more my simply going away, then my being hatefully taken.   Because I was seventy four, so it was time for me to die.   And I had long been seriously ill, so I was ready to die. But then we all die, though some too soon, while others not soon enough. And finally death became something for my heart to rest upon.

There was little in my life that I held as sacred for any length of time. But in spite of this indifference, the many years were not all bad. I can list the things I wanted to do but failed at, the things I could have done but did not, and list the things that succeeded quite well. But the last of my life was not as spectacular as the first of my life. But then beginnings on the scale I chose are always spectacular.

In New York City, I was a member of the firm of Appleton - Century-Crofts, and later J. B. Lippincott Company.   Then for the last ten years of my life I conducted a Book Review Column in newspapers throughout the South and the Mid-West. But just as writers who can no longer write, teach, so to, editors who can no longer edit, review. It is rather like studs being put in the next pastures to the mares after they can no longer stud.

During the Depression of the thirties, though, I started an avant garde magazine in the Village, and for several years it well represented the vangard of the then new literature. But the creditors eventually closed it when the revenues never did equal the expenses. But the magazine was a spectacular success because it reflected exactly what I had intended and what was needed. And I was a spectacular success among the then writers of the Village because I had provided them with an outlet to the reading public however small and briefly. But it continued to puzzle me where the creditors got the idea that the magazine would ever make a profit. Because some things should exist simply because they must. And because the brave are not supposed to pause to consider.

In hindsight, everything that came after the magazine was anti-climatic, even though it did not seem so at the time. The magazine became my carte blanche to the then publishing world of the City, and I was respected and welcomed wherever I went without ever being known personally. And for those next years it became quite the fashion for us to assault everything of the status quo, while embracing everything of the revolutionary. But once you have torn everything down that is flimsy, without having substantial replacements, the results is a large void. And even as we called names, we were being called names, without there being a judge to decide which of us were right. So finally it had become just a silly game, like a mean trick that we had played upon ourselves, and so we quit it and got jobs.

Of the little in my life that I held as sacred, I held womanhood as sacred for probably the longest. But back then it was quite natural for young men to place women on pedestals. And until their brittleness won out finally, it was a proper location indeed for them. I married a beautiful woman who was above me socially. Apparently she believed the expectations about me that still were in circulation even that long after the magazine ceased. And she must have thought that one day I would locate on a pedestal beside her. When I did not, she spent the next years in confusion with one foot on the pedestal and the other foot off. And I spent the next years feeling that I owed her some sort of an apology. I enjoyed her very much off the pedestal though. But I felt that she did not really like having such private things done to an idol in the night. My middle years were financially comfortable, and now and then exciting, and always lonely. But I had learned to at least not be an embarrassment.

A book only becomes a book, when it is published. Until then it is a manuscript. And, too, an author only becomes an author, when he is published. Until then he is a writer. So publication is everything. Just as being commercial is everything. Because there will be no publications unless the writer, and therefore the manuscript, is commercial. But many are called, but few are chosen, as the saying goes. And if an author is not completely commercial with his first book, he will be on the subsequent books, because greed and self preservation have a way of rationalizing everything while they make strangers of friends.

During my years in the pasture, the New York publishers continually supplied me with an endless flow of review books, as did the small presses and the regional presses. Because publicity and promotion are everything in publishing. These I dutifully read and reviewed as fairly and objectively as I could for the strictly commercial ventures that they were. Then I gave this endless flow of boxes of books to libraries and to family and to friends, until they, too, became inundated with books and would have no more. Then I would stop strangers on the street and say in a husky and secretive voice, "hey, you wanta box of books?" And as an old man, that gave me a strange pleasure.

During those years, also, it was my good fortune to receive several unusual books from several rather desperate authors. Unusual books in that they certainly were not commercial ventures. Desperate authors in that they each had formed their own small presses to publish their own books after none of the established publishers would. If there had been a touch of vanity publishing in the self publication of their first books, this surely ceased with the self publication of their second, then third, then fourth books. Because book publishing is terribly expensive, and only the most determined and dedicated would persevere under such horrendous financial losses. Apparently these desperate authors drew their courage from some well that has no name. And in time I came to know each of them fairly well from their books and letters, and from their determination. So I introduced them to each other by a personal note from me, since they were from various parts of the country and could never possibly meet, so they at least would have someone similar to correspond with when I died on some today that then was still in the future.

In their unusual books, these desperate authors were certain that they were writing magnificent book worlds of gold door handles and silver bells, and characters who speak as honey glistens. But

you. Just as stewardesses mostly wait on you and clean up after you. But we do not mention this to our charter boat captains. Because we do not like to see grown men sulk and whimper and pout.

They are the ones with the 'I'd rather be deep sea fishing' stickers on their bumpers and the 'Ducks Unlimited' decals on the rear windows of their vehicles. Although we have yet to figure out what unlimited ducks have to do with charter fishing. But somehow they seem to derive a great deal of pride out of such displays. And what is the harm anyway? They are the ones who are always sitting at tables off to themselves in our bars. In ones and twos and threes, there so silent and so strong and so secretive. There protecting their desired image even as they project it. They who wait on you and clean up after you, for the romance of it and for the mystic of it, and for a rather stiff fee of course. But you are too hung-over grey to care about all this when you board their sleek vessels at dawn. And you are too seasick green to care about all this when after a seeming eternity of upchucking misery you are returned finally to the marinas unmoving dock. Where faster than a speeding bullet, you abandon them to us, for us to once again tolerate and humor as best as we can.

Because commercial fishermen grunt everyday, and almost all day. Whether we want to or not. Because that is what it is to be a commercial fisherman. But charter boat captains do not like to grunt. No, not at all. And they refuse to grunt, until it becomes absolutely necessary and positively unavoidable. Because to them, charter boat captains simply were not put on this earth to grunt.

Just as the truly beautiful stewardesses do not feel that they were put on this earth to sweat. Because by rights they, each, have far more distinguished and far more elevated things to do. So it is with great reluctance and after many delays and after every possible excuse, that in their off season winters, when even the most avid of you off shore fishermen stay home warm and comfortable by the fireside to play with the baby's mother, that our charter boat captains do finally load forty or fifty or sixty sea bass pots onto their sleek vessels in a yes belated and almost serious and certainly desperate rush to respond to the increasingly frequent and the harshly vocal demands of the Bank. The always impersonal Bank, that does not care in the least about images or birthrights or grunts or the truly beautiful.

And so, like condemned men on their way to the gallows, the grim faced charter boat captains leave the marinas at dawn every morning, sentenced to the all day of grunting that is in the pulling and the working of a bunch of sea bass pots. Gone are the suntans. Gone is the glamour. Gone is the mystery. Gone is the romance. Here is only the wet cold angry windy rolling winter sea. Because sea bass, unlike clients, do not need to have their egos massaged. And sea bass, again unlike clients, do not in turn massage the egos of our charter boat captains. Because the sea bass is a fish, and only a fish, and they do not expect to be waited upon, or to be cleaned up after. And when back at the marinas, the sea bass do not then stand about in quickly dispersing boisterous groups of shouted rounds of handshakes and of the bravado of who made the biggest catch and 'we'll do it again real soon'. And worst of all, the sea bass do not leave large tips.

But in the evenings in our bars, the charter boat captains stoically remain true to their created selves and to their desired images, in spite of their day of grunting humiliation and degradation. There still sitting off to themselves by ones or two or threes. There still protecting even as they project. While from the stools at the crowded wood bars, we shout our good natured harassments at them unmercifully so they will not feel quite so unloved and quite so unappreciated. Because we really do love them. And we really do appreciate them. Because the marinas and the waterfront and our bars would be far less exciting and interesting without them. The charter boat captains. There in their battery warmed thick socks beneath their scruffy sneakers and their brushed denim pants and their big weave wool sweaters with plaid scarves tight about their necks and a Ben Hogan golf cap pulled low over their eyes. Now is that any way for commercial fishermen to dress in winter? But spring is near. And spring is coming. And with spring will come charters. And with charters they again can be the men they so want to be when they grow up.

WE SCALLOPED TODAY

We scalloped today,
   David and me,

      we labored today,
      here beside the sea.

It was a January day,
the kind we always dread,
      it was a cruel day,
      with a low sky grey and dead.

Our clumsy hands were numb,
our noses ran nasty wet,
      our teary eyes were glazed,
      our mouths cold grim set.

But our season is every Monday and Wednesday,
however they are,
      and our reason is money for bills and expenses,
      though it won't go far.

Everything was movement,
there on the stern deck of the skiff,
      everything was action,
      hauling in the heavy drags to lift.

The water kept a rough chop,
the wind blew a stiff gale,
        the skiff kept a constant roll,
        the motor throbbed a steady wail.

While one drag grassed up,
the other muddied up,
        with us battling the two,
        without let up.

High tide never made,
low all the day,
        we bumped and we grounded,
        and the wind never lay.

Over the shallow shoals,
where the hell's the channel?,
        up on the shelly rocks,
        there ain't no damn channel!

Long dragging the drags,
 hard hauling in the drags,
        fast dumping the grassy mud we had drug,
        slow culling the awful mess we had drug,

Thirty bushels the daily limit,
fifteen for each,

      grinding out this days load,
      taking forever to reach.

When late afternoon to the buyer,
wallowed we, six dollars per, from the dock said he,
where's last weeks eight dollars?, moan cried we,

      same place as two weeks agoes ten dollars,
      replied he,   but when he turned his back, in
      your goddamn pocket!,
      mumble cursed we.

We scalloped today,
David and me,

      we labored today,
      here beside the sea.

SOMETHING FOR LITERATURE

Writing something for literature is like building a grand fence with homemade bricks, without the aid of a brick mold or a bubble level or a leveling string. Each day you mix the materials for that day's brick, then you very carefully shape that brick. When you have finished, and if the materials have been properly mixed, and if the brick has been properly shaped, then you skillfully place it alongside the other bricks in your under construction fence. But if the materials have not been properly mixed, or if the brick has not been properly shaped, then you toss that brick onto the pile of other culled bricks, and tomorrow you begin all over again. In fact, either way, tomorrow you always begin all over again. And it is only after the hard work of a great many days of individually mixing and individually shaping and individually placing that your fence can be constructed. But it is only when the last brick has been skillfully placed, that your fence can be called completed. Only then can you stand away from your fence to see whether all the daily homemade bricks really do combine to produce a grand fence. If so, then you have written something for literature. If not, then you go to a different site, and tomorrow you begin again to mix the materials for a single brick.

AND THEN THERE WERE NONE

There are very few fishing villages remaining now that have not become something else also because of economics. Swansboro has certainly become something else also because of economics. It has pretty well become a bedroom village of people who work at jobs in the towns that are fifteen to twenty or more miles away. Because these people prefer to live here because it is still small and still quiet, and of course because it is beside the water. And during spring and summer and fall Swansboro becomes very much a village of tourists and vacationers. But only last is it a fishing village now. And not really much of a fishing village at that, not anymore. Not anything like what it had been. Because for all of its long history it was a very important fishing village indeed. That and only that. A village of fishermen and their families. That is until recently.

And the Jolly Roger down near the docks is the last remaining bar around here that is still for fishermen only. But soon it will be forced to become something else also because of economics. But for now and for awhile yet it will continue to be exactly what it has always been. And there is comfort in that. Because we enjoy going there very much, and we are quite protective of it, so we do not mention it when we are around outsiders because we do not want to lose it too. But I did not enjoy going to the Jolly Roger when I first moved to Swansboro and began to become a commercial clammer. Because the fishermen were quite protective of it then too, and maybe more so, and I was an outsider to them, so they ignored me almost to the point of hostility. But I went there now and then anyway, and I weathered their hostility and being ignored and not enjoying myself there, all because of a strong personal need to hear them and to be around them and to one day be one of them.

Because fishermen are fiercely proud men, and I have always greatly admired this attitude in men. But for the work that fishermen do and where they do that work and the conditions under which they do that work and the amount that they get paid for that work, fishermen certainly must be the least respected workmen of all workmen. But they remain fiercely proud men anyway. Proud to the point of hatred toward change, and proud to the point of hostility toward outsiders. But grudgingly and over much time I finally earned the name fisherman from them. So now we call each other "capt'n", and I am very welcome at the Jolly Roger.

But when I began no one would tell me or show me how to do commercial clamming correctly. So for the first year I not only did everything wrong, I did very little that was right, or even close to being right. So I remember that year as being a very long year that was filled with frustration and loneliness and discouragement. But I stuck with it. And even though I gave up a thousand times during that very long year, I did not quit and go somewhere else to do something else. But my not quitting was really more a case of my not having any other choice, rather than my being decisive and courageous and dedicated. Because I had come to Swansboro completely wrecked emotionally and wiped out financially and a

179

real mess spiritually. So it had been a fleeing escape and a humiliating defeat and a one last resort all together in a desperate lunge to hide and to be safe. So there was very much of the hang dog tail between his legs woe begone aspect to my whole atmosphere and appearance. And in hindsight and in fairness to the other fishermen, I probably would not have wanted to associate with a man who looked as absolutely pathetic as I looked either.

I would later learn that back then clamming was what the fishermen resorted to when they had become ruined at shrimping or at fishing, or when a major mechanical breakdown caused them to lose their trawlers to foreclosure. Because with a skiff of some kind and an outboard motor of some kind and a clam rake of some kind, or simply walking out along the banks and hand clamming on all fours, anyone could become a commercial clammer. Because that was what you could do when utter survival and making it through just one more day was what brutally faced you. When because of luck or because of stupidity, you had hit bottom literally and considering your momentum had probably gone somewhat beyond bottom. So anything that you did, even if it was done wrong, would be a step up. Because finally up was the only direction that you could go, because you had already gone as far down as you could. And the fishermen called this bottoming out. You had bottomed out, and could now begin again.

So I had bottomed out. But the roller coaster ride down had been one hell of a ride for sure. But the return ride would not be anywhere as fast or as direct or as simple. The some kind of a skiff that I got was a far too narrow freshwater boat that definitely was not suited to the frequently rough saltwater of the bays and the rivers and the sounds that are all around Swansboro. The some kind of an outboard motor that I got was a young person's pair of far too short oars. And for that first year I literally rowed my ass off. My ass which before had tended toward puny anyway, soon became an ass that was little more than a skeleton with some poor skin hung on it. But it did not take many weeks before my ass became hard, though quite slight still, just as my stomach became hard, and my arms and my wrists and my back and my hands became hard also. And in the process I learned more about myself, the real myself, than I had ever before known, and certainly more than I really wanted to know at the time. Because it is not at all pleasant to confront the stark and the exact you without any coverings and without any make up. I learned that when you are on saltwater each day in all weather and whichever season, you damn well better learn to think smart and to think for yourself because no one is with you to think for you smart or otherwise. And from this I learned that if you are man enough to leave the dock in a boat of whatever size, you damn well better be man enough to bring that boat safely back to the dock whatever may happen and usually does. And from these I began to learn winds and tides and weather, and how to use them whenever I could and when to run from them whenever I couldn't. It was a hell of a hard education all right, out there everyday where there are no textbooks or professors or classrooms, and yet a vast schoolhouse of vital things to learn. And graduation was when you had the pure shit scared out of you and lived to tell about it, and you couldn't wait to get out and face it all again the next day.

The some kind of a clam rake that I got was a fifteen dollar plus tax cheapee pearake that are sold in supermarkets to tourist clammers who do not know what they are doing. And with the change from that last twenty I bought a ten pound bag of potatoes and two packs of cigarettes. And I had a dime and a nickel and four pennies remaining to jingle in my pocket so I would not have the lost wanderer feeling of being dead broke miserable. So I would have fried potatoes for meals and a cigarette now and then for entertainment until I began making money from clamming, however many days that that required.

Before I left the dock early the next morning I stopped a guy at the marina and asked him what a clam looked like and where I might find some. He looked at me for a long minute, eagerly standing there with the paint still unscratched on my brand new supermarket pearake. He blinked his eyes a bunch of times, then shook his head sadly, then he blinked his eyes a bunch more times. Finally he asked if I had seen the signs out-front of Shell filling stations. Of course I said yes right away, knowing immediately what a clam looked like. But he said that that was a scallop, not a clam. So I said oh and my face fell. But he continued anyway and said that scallops move around on top of the bottom, while clams were in the bottom and did not move around; That the two looked somewhat similar, but that clams had smooth shells and were thicker through the middle. So I said all right with some enthusiasm, because with this crucial information firmly grasped my eagerness had begun to trickle back. Then I asked him where there was a bottom that clams might be in. He blinked his eyes a bunch of times again, then said for me to go to that bay yonder and try along the bank and I probably would find some. So I looked yonder where he had pointed to be certain I had the right bay, and so I would know what a bay looked like. I said there and he said yep, and with my eagerness now fully restored, I could not thank him enough. But he only shook his head sadly, and then walked away.

So I rowed across to the bay and began to pearake in the sandy mud that was along the bank, in a very serious search for my first clam. Seven hours later my hands were blistered and my arms felt like lead weights, and I did not think that my back would straighten so I could ever again walk upright. But in addition to the first clam, I had seventeen more. But at ten cents each that was only a dollar and eighty cents for seven hours of the hottest and the stinkingest and the hardest work that I had ever done. And I was too ashamed to take only eighteen clams to the buyer. So I kept them in saltwater in my tub in my rowboat overnight. But the next day I only got twenty clams for a two day total of thirty eight. And I was still too ashamed to go to the buyer even though three dollars and eighty cents would buy a pretty good chunk of some kind of meat, and I had already enjoyed fried potatoes for about as long as I could stand. Then the third day I hit the mother lode for sure, because I got one hundred and ten clams and right away peed in my pants from the excitement of it all. Because one hundred and forty eight clams was fourteen dollars and eighty cents, so my too ashamed suddenly vanished, because that night I would definitely have my fill of meat and beer then chain smoke a pack of cigarettes if I wanted to because I had damn well earned it.

Well, the work never did get any easier, but before long I developed a stamina for it. And after the first few days I no longer noticed the stink of the mud and the marshes and the clams and the saltwater. The cool of the fall was nice after the heat of the summer, but then harsh winter came and I nearly froze to death while praying for spring. But I had gotten much better at finding clams, because I was regularly bringing in one hundred and fifty to two hundred a day, and fifteen to twenty dollars a day is all the money in the world when you have just bottomed out. But every afternoon at the buyer I could see that the real commercial clammers were regularly bringing in eight hundred to a thousand clams, and quite often more. And this astounded me, and it made me envious, and it was discouraging. Because if they would not even nod to acknowledge my presence, much less return my hello, then they sure as hell would not tell me where they got so many clams or how they got them.

Because for all those months back then I felt like the invisible man. I knew that I was living and breathing and actually there among them, but they did not seem to. They would look right through me and they would talk right through me, and if I did not step out of the way in the nick of time they would have walked right through me. But I continued to row out then row in each day anyway, and gradually I ventured farther and farther from the dock and tried the next bay or the next mudflat or the next slough. And I did everything wrong and I could do very little that was right, and what I learned was always learned the hard way and the slow way. But I watched and I listened and I asked questions however dumb they might be, and every evening I made a list of the things I had learned that day and what things I wanted to learn the next day.

It was one day about a year after I had begun that a commercial clammer spoke to me for the first time. Because I guess it takes that long for you to begin to be visible to them. I was working a point of land down the inland waterway from Swansboro when one of them came roaring by in his broad skiff with a big outboard on the stern. He idled down suddenly then yelled to me that I was clamming in a closed area, and if the Fisheries man caught me he would give me a ticket and make me dump my clams. Well right away I felt spotlighted in a bank vault at night, and I stuttered something about not knowing. He said a storm must have knocked down the sign, but that everyone knew where the closed line was. So now I felt dumb in addition to quilty. He pointed to the next point of land and said that it wasn't closed, that it had been worked pretty well, but that there should still be clams there if I wanted to try it. So I let out a string of yeahs and sures and you bets and thank yous and appreciate its and much obligeds like he was Santa Claus and it was Christmas Eve. Well, I got five hundred clams off the point of land that he sent me to that day. So right away I peed in my pants again. Because clams were bringing twelve cents then, and I made sixty dollars in one day and had begun to be visible too. So I was off and running, and nothing could stop me now.

By the middle of that second year I had saved two thousand dollars, the hard way of course and the slow way of course, by five dollars or ten dollars a day or twenty or thirty dollars a day as often as I could. Until finally it seemed as though I had all the money in the world stacked in that old jewelry box. So the next morning I went down to the marina and paid seventeen hundred and fifty dollars for a brand new flat bottom fiberglass work skiff, and two hundred and fifty dollars for a fourth hand twenty horse outboard that the then owner guaranteed would crank and get me away from the dock. But how far away he couldn't say, and whether it would get me back to the dock he wouldn't guarantee. So with my new skiff launched and the twenty horse mounted on her stern, I had a long private talk with my precious outboard. I told her how far I had come toward becoming a commercial clammer since bottoming out, and how very far I still had to go. I told her that I would clean her up squeaking clean, and that I would paint her nice and bright. That I would keep only new spark plugs in her, and use only the best oil and gas mixture. That I would keep her well greased, and would check her lower unit once a month. That I would take good care of her. And that in return I wanted her to take good care of me out there everyday where harm is real and sudden and always close. And I did, and she did, and I rowed no more. Because I was off and running, and nothing could stop me now.

And now that where I could work was no longer severely limited by the out and in distance that I could row, then I was free to travel to all of the bays and rivers and sounds that are around Swansboro. And even surmount a hard blowing wind and fast running tide, which was the ultimate freedom to me. And with this mobility then I began to regularly bring in five to six hundred clams a day. So I invested one hundred dollars in a bullrake to work the shelly areas, because the commercial clammers used bullrakes and they regularly doubled me. And one by one they began to return my wave when we passed each other in our skiffs. And at the buyer they would return my hello, because I was becoming more visible to them by the week. So I invested fifty dollars in a long handle for my bullrake so I could work from my skiff during high tides when the water was too high to work overboard, because I saw that that was what they did. Then I invested one hundred dollars in a set of tongs to work the patches of shells that were too small an area to work with the long handle, because they did that also. And they called me by name now when I came to the buyer. And more and more often they invited me to come work where they were working. So reluctantly but out of necessity for the additional power, I sold my dependable twenty horse for four hundred dollars, then added another four hundred dollars to that and bought a thirty five horse that was only second hand. And when I came into the Jolly Roger now they would motion for me to come sit with them. Because finally I had become one of them. And even though my frequent questions still showed my ignorance and my lack of experience, they answered each question openly and at length and they did not make me feel dumb. And by being well equipped now and fairly well skilled now, and by being one of them now, then that next year would be the happiest and the most satisfying of the years that I was a commercial clammer.

It was during the next year, this past year, that several of us who were more ambitious began to haul out our skiffs onto boat trailers and to travel to other areas of North Carolina in the hope of finding an area where clamming was better than it had become around Swansboro. Because there had been so many people clamming around here for so many years that those of us who did it full time now were just barely surviving at it. And we hoped that the same was not true in these other areas, and that there would be at least one area remaining where we could once again make a decent living at the work that we did best. But the same was true wherever we went, and sometimes even worse, but we did not know that yet and this was what we would learn that year. Because hope is as much a part of being a commercial clammer as anything else.

We had good days in the shelly places that are in the Straits that run between Harkers Island and Marshallburg. Then in the shelly places around Browns Island and behind Shackleford Banks and toward Cape Lookout. And we received the immediate attention of everyone who was there at the ramps where we launched. Because they knew from our work skiffs and our equipment and from our entire appearance that we were professionals, and that we had arrived on very serious business indeed. But our receptions were always ones of silent resentment rather than ones of warm welcome. Because we had come to harvest a resource which they felt was theirs alone and therefore did not belong to outsiders. So we quickly began to be referred to all along the coast as "those goddamn clammers from Swansboro".

But we drew pride from this disparagement because we were the best and we knew that we were the best, and because we were dedicated and because we were efficient. Because we were young and strong and skilled. Because we truly were commercial clammers.

We had good days in the shallows and the cuts and the shoals that are beside the deepwater channel at Southport, where the huge ocean going tankers and container ships slid only a half a mile away by us and dwarfed us giant beside child pitifully out there in our oh so frail and tiny skiffs. We had good days on the long shelly reefs that butt and crisscross and combine to form Shell Castle that is so weather vulnerable there in the middle of Ocracoke Inlet with the thriving tourist village of Ocracoke in one direction and the hundred year abandoned ghost town of Portsmouth in the other direction, and with the vast Pamplico Sound sweeping to the far horizon and beyond behind it all the way from South to West to North and to North East. We had good days in the many small sounds and bays and creeks and sloughs that go one into the other the length behind Wrightsville Beach and Carolina Beach and Kure Beach then to the Inland Waterway. And we had good days in the just hard sand and in the grassy hard sand that begins at Core Banks themselves and runs far out into Core Sound then for mile after mile from Cedar Island to Atlantic to Sealevel then on to Stacy and to Davis. And even though we already had learned to have a wary respect for the rough water that the Pamplico Sound could produce, we quickly learned to have an equally wary respect for the rough water that Core Sound could

189

produce as well. And for the very few minutes that it took for her to produce it. Because for every scare that the Pamplico Sound gave us, Core Sound matched its scare for scare and intensity for intensity. Until being rough water skiff capable no longer was enough, we had to be rough water skiff wise also.

But always there were the bad days. Always and ever these, and again and again. Days when fast traveling cold fronts moved in and the water quickly went from mirror slick calm to white capped swelled from winds that battered us until working in it became impossible. Days when high tide was expected, but because of the combination of moon phase and low pressure and wind direction a sudden flood tide resulted, with the water two to three feet above normal and therefore unworkable. And we could only stand frustrated at the roads' end and stare silently at the flooded water under which the ramp somewhere was. And on these days, these too too many bad days, we could only return to Swansboro dejected and discouraged and broker than when we had left.

And the bad days of endless looking. Looking here, looking there, looking everywhere. But not finding. Because the army had been there before us. And this was true wherever we went during that year. The army always had been there before us. And the good days, the few good days, had come only because we were more skilled and more determined and better equipped than the army. But even with these advantages, all that we really did was clean out the spots and the pockets and the corners that the army had missed or could not get to or did not know how to work. So then we knew that there simply was not any place along the coast that we as professionals could move to and through conservation and proper harvesting make a decent living. Because the army of part time clammers had already been everywhere and still was everywhere and would continue to be everywhere. This while there still is no one, no department, no agency, not even the beginning of a management philosophy to stop them or to reduce them or even to control them. And this with a resource that is so dynamic in its renewability that only through complete and shameful and intentional stupidity could it become reduced to the barrenness that it now is and to the extinction that it very soon will be.

So last month one of us hauled his skiff and parked it in his backyard. Then he got a job as a soft drink truck driver. And he will develop and improve his route in time, then he will make a decent living at that. Last week another of us hauled his skiff and parked it in his backyard. Then he began to do fiberglass repair work on boats. And since there already are a lot of powerboats and houseboats and sailboats around Swansboro, with more arriving each year, he will make a decent living at that.

So yesterday afternoon me and Larry sat on stools at the bar at the Jolly Roger, and looked at our wind blown and saltwater crusty selves in the smoke dimmed mirror beyond. And he asked me how I had done and where I had clammed. Then I asked him the same. But neither of us really listened to the other's answer. Because it did not matter, nor would it make a difference. So we finished those draughts and Rita brought refills, because refills come right away now at the Jolly. Because it isn't anything like it use to be at this time of day with commercial clammers steadily coming in by ones and twos, all excited and happy and can't wait for tomorrow, and Rita steadily refilling draughts one after the other. So an outsider can't even get ignored to the point of hostility here anymore. Because there is so few of us now to do it, and what for anyway?

Then Larry said, "Well, we're making fifty bucks a day. And that ain't bad."

"Hell, that's not money, Larry, and you know it."

And he knew it. And I knew it. And the others of us knew it too, and that is why they have gotten out. Because fifty bucks a day for three hundred and fifty days is only seventeen fifty for the year. But with the bad days subtracted we don't even make close to three hundred days. So now you're talking way less than fifteen for the year. And boat fuel comes off the top of that, as does outboard maintenance and boat maintenance and equipment maintenance. Plus putting aside some for upgrading these whenever we can. And we ain't even started talking about everyday living expenses yet. Naw, fifty bucks a day ain't shit. Not today. Not ever again. But it's great money for the army of part timers though, because they already have good incomes from elsewhere. So it's just farting around money to them, extras money, getting ahead money, load up the wife and kids and grandma too and get out on the water fun money. And they will ride this plunder train to the end of the ravished line, without a second thought, without a single care. And when the raped end comes they will just shrug and stroll away whistling, because it was great pillage while it lasted.

But we care until we want to cry, is how much we care. Lord how we do care. And we care until it is breaking our hearts, is how much we care. And that death in the family feeling is the dull ache that we carry always with us now. Because working from a skiff on the water through all the seasons is what we want to do above anything else and beyond everything else. Because with becoming a commercial clammer comes a respect for the clam that becomes an awe. Because the clam is a truly fine sea animal that is well adapted and well suited and fiercely proud and fiercely determined. Because the clam is indeed a worthy harvest for a worthy professional. And to be a forced witness to the stripped destruction of its populations is as terrible a hurt as a caring man will ever know.

So I thought of the hard years that it took for me to become a commercial clammer. Of all those first days of rowing out and rowing in. Of all the sunrises and the sunsets. Of all the warm gorgeous days and all the cold stormy days. Of all those sad lonely months when I did everything wrong, and could do very little that was right. Until ever so slowly gradually becoming strong enough and equipped enough and man enough to finally become a skilled craftsman at a very difficult trade. Until finally becoming skiff wise and tide wise and weather wise and clam wise, only to painfully learn that I can no longer and never again make a decent living at this trade. That merely surviving at it is the most that I can expect now, and this for only a year longer. If that long. So a man can't even bottom out around here anymore. And do the honest productive work that is so soothing so rewarding while he picks up the shattered prices of his shattered self, and begins the sure process toward becoming a more durable and a more reliable man. Now they will have to do something else, because of economics. Just as we now will have to do something else, because of economics. But what a terrible hurt it truly is for a caring man.

"What else would you do?" Larry asked.

"I was doing home repair work before. But got too much of it on account and not enough in cash, and went broke. I could start that again. But run it better."

"Clamming is all I've ever done. All I know. Nine years now. Even left high school to do it. But clams were thick everywhere then. And we didn't think it would ever end."

"I came too late. Then it took me too long to learn. So all I saw was the last of it."

"Hell, we were bringing in fifteen hundred, two thousand clams a day. No problem. Just put in the hours."

"Those days are gone."

"Yeah, they're gone. But we were proud men for a lot of years."

Yes they were. Then for awhile, yes we were. But not now. Not ever again here. But I did not want it to end. Now that I had only just begun. But it was over. It really was over. And I did not have a choice. And I could only delay for however long or short, before going ahead and doing what I had to do. Like knowing that eventually you would have to bite a hateful bullet, but putting that off again and again, before finally going ahead and biting it. And Larry does not have a choice either. Because last week his wife told him that she is pregnant. And a man alone can handle mere survival. And sometimes a man and his wife can handle mere survival. But a man cannot put his child through mere survival. Not and still be a man. Naw, Larry does not have a choice. But yesterday at the Jolly Roger he still wanted to think that he did.

DREAM

The trick where you imagine that your eyes are at the sharp edges of the pearake teeth as they cut their way through the sand and the shell and the eel grass bottom in search of clams is not working very well this evening because your concentration keeps drifting in and out because it already has been a way too long day in this cold and in this wind. But nine hundred clams is better than eight hundred clams and is ten dollars more at ten cents each at the buyer and you have already tricked yourself into going for the next hundred clams for four days so far this week so when you finally do get the next hundred clams today that will be five days and an additional fifty dollars more onto your pay for the week that you would not have otherwise.

And you will clam tomorrow of course and if you once again trick yourself into staying for the next hundred then that will be sixty dollars more for the week and taking this further that will be two hundred and forty dollars more for the month and taking this further still that will be three thousand one hundred and twenty dollars more for the year. But you already know to not spend that until you make that, yes, you already know that very well indeed. But these are simply more of the many tricks that you have learned to use to overcome the fatigue and to overcome the loneliness and to overcome the monotony that is so much a part of being a commercial clammer out here alone everyday from spring to summer to fall to winter to spring again. And after all of these years of doing this for a living the days simply blur together into one long blurry day stream of doing this for a living yes they do. And that is about all it amounts to is a living yes it does. But then every day is different with the every day different tide and different wind and different weather until even all those differences become everyday because since everything is different every day then even that becomes everyday within itself as well. But you promised yourself that when the fun and the excitement and the challenge stopped that you would stop doing this kind of fishing and you would go do another kind of fishing. But you do not remember when the fun and the excitement and the challenge stopped, you simply know that they stopped a long time ago but still you have kept doing this kind of fishing because this kind of fishing has become what you do and who you are. So you have kept doing this kind of fishing because another kind of fishing would lose its fun and its' excitement and its' challenge too in time and then you would be doing that kind of fishing because that would be the kind of fishing that you do and who you are. So you may as well keep doing this kind of fishing because after awhile all kinds of fishing come down to simply the fatigue and the loneliness and the monotony of it.

And even this way of thinking is really one more trick among the many tricks that you use to trick yourself into coming out here everyday to clam one more day and then one more day and then one more day while each day you trick yourself into staying for the next hundred clams and then the next hundred clams until all that it has become is simply a whole bunch of little tricks that you keep playing on yourself until it all has become simply one big trick that you play on yourself all day everyday. Still, this kind of fishing, or any kind of fishing really, sure beats the hell out of a hill job any hill job until there is no comparison because you have done the hill job thing yes hell you have and you sure as hell don't want to do the hill job thing again no hell you don't. And you have to make a living doing something even if it is only just a living. And this is how you have picked to make your living even though it is only just a living. Because a family is expensive. Because Christina is expensive because women are that, expensive. Because the maintenance of a wood shrimp boat comes with a woman and Christina proves that point. Just as the maintenance of a wood shrimp boat comes with kids and Brad and C.J. proves that point. So you have to make a living at something even if it is only just a living because the maintenance of a wood shrimp boat comes with just living yes hell it does. But the trick where you imagine that your eyes are at the sharp edges of the pearake as they cut their way through the sand and the shell and the eel grass bottom in search of clams is definitely not working any longer any more this evening because by now your concentration is definitely shot and gone because of this way too long day out here in this cold and in this wind.

But now you look up and see that your skiff is loose and is going with the wind across Pamplico Sound. No! But how can this be?! Because there is the rod that you use for a stake still jammed in the shelly grassy bottom. But now you see that it is leaned far over. So the two half hitches of the bowline simply slid along the rod until they slid off when the rod was leaned that far over. But how can this be?! Now you realize how strong and getting stronger this northeast wind has become. Strong enough for the pull of your skiff in this strong wind to lean the rod far over. But when did this start while you were concentrating so on your various tricks?! Now you realize that the incoming tide that just was knee deep is now almost waist deep and is rising still. And that the water surface is quickly going from blown chops to bulky swells. But how can this be?! Now you realize that there is no way in hell that you can wade run fast enough to catch your skiff. Because this strong northeast wind already has it scudding along and heading into the open Pamplico Sound with nothing to stop it until it beaches itself on the mainland shore five miles away way across yonder. No! But how can this be?!

Now you see another pearaker in the evening dimness that is now well on its way to becoming night darkness, there way up from you with Ocracoke Inlet much farther still. But with the distance he and his skiff are only separate small silhouettes, here behind remote Portsmouth Island that is so barrien that you can far away hear the surf pound over on the ocean side. Then you see his silhouette blur with the silhouette of his skiff. Then you see his silhouette atop the silhouette of his skiff. Now at the stern you see him quickly lean down and then suddenly rare back as he gives his outboard pull cord a sharp pull. Now you see the combined still small silhouette of him atop his skiff begin to race the wind over and along the choppy bulky swells and then out into the open Pamplico Sound. But he does not know that your skiff is loose and is racing the wind ahead of him also. But he does not even know that you have been clamming way down from him. No! But how can this be?!

Now you realize too late that this northeaster had been building itself all along to the deep ocean of the beachside of Portsmouth Island during the most of the day ebb tide. But by mid-afternoon when the tide turned to flood tide it came ahead and it surged itself to inshore to here together with this hard blowing gale. Now you look and see that the shore of the backside of Portsmouth Island is three hundred yards away. No! Because the water is already above your waist and rising still. Because there is no way in hell that you can wade to that backside shore in these waders and with all these heavy clothes on and against such blowing swells with the water already this deep. No! But how can this be?!

Because now you realize that you are drowned! Because now you realize that you are crab bait! Because you let yourself get distracted by your various daily tricks of another hundred clams another hundred clams. Because you let yourself get distracted by the fatigue and the monotony and the loneliness that is in this fishery that is in all fisheries. Because you forgot the seriousness of what it is that you do for a living even though it is only just a living. But mainly it is because you forgot the seriousness of where it is that you make this living that is only just a living. Because you have long known that the sea quickly kills those who forget those who forget even briefly. So now she has killed you.

But then this was only a terrible dream of several seconds in the way late of a restless night. Or was it a prediction of the future?

TROOP TRAINS

I was in the Eighth Grade and my world was my best buddies and playing games and running and jumping and tussling and horse playing and looking for mischief wherever we could find it. And since mischief was everywhere, we were not far behind it.

My Dad was an Electrician at the Camp Lejeune Marine Base on the coast in North Carolina. And we lived in a large oval housing project named Midway Park, and all of the Dads worked on Base as Carpenters and Plumbers and Painters and Mechanics and whatever. Across the road was the Main Gate into the Base. That road went fifteen miles to the fishing village of Swansboro in one direction, and five miles to the Town of Jacksonville in the other direction. Camp Lejeune was the Marine Base for the East Coast, just as Camp Pendleton was the Marine Base for the West Coast.

So my Eighth Grade world existed within the larger world of Marines and the Marine Corps. My school was on Base and my school bus driver was a Marine and I had an I.D. card and the band for my schools' special events came from the Marine Corps Band. And during the summer I sometimes sold newspapers to Marines at their Mess Halls at dawn. So seeing Marines parading and Marines at P.T. and Marines on maneuvers and Marines at the live fire range and Marines running in formation and Marines running always running along the roadways was a normal background in my world.

Me and my best buddies even found a trail through the pine woods from Midway Park to a large war gear dump on Base, where ammo cartridge belts and pup tents and back packs and K rations and canned rations and gas masks and cartons of Lucky Strikes and a hundred other war gear things were boxed and and stacked and left over from World War Two. But one puff of a long dried Lucky Strike was enough for us of the cigarette mischief. Just as having the Military Police walking up the walkway to our homes to talk to us was enough of our war gear dump visiting mischief.

Then one afternoon the newspaper headline screamed that the North Korean Army had swarmed down across the 38th Parallel into South Korea and were already spreading out across the width of the Korean Peninsula in mass. That they could push our army there down and down and further down into the sea even. And it was that suddenly that my before world was simply brushed aside as though it had never existed. I stopped playing and went inside to listen to the radio news broadcast. I studied the Korean Peninsula map on the front page of the newspaper that showed where the North Korean Army already was, and where our Army's line already was. And it already seemed hopeless. So it was just that quickly that my new world became the radio news broadcasts and the newspaper front pages and the troop trains.

The Atlantic Coastline Railroad had several railroad beds that ran side by side mostly beside Highway 17 down the width of North Carolina. But at the Jacksonville junction, there was only one spur railroad that ran the five miles to the Main Gate and then deep into Camp Lejeune. Which meant that only one train of passenger cars and flatcars could be on the spur at a time. But the panic was to get all of the Marines and all of their gear and all of their equipment the three thousand miles with the green light all the way from Camp Lejeune on the East Coast to Camp Pendleton on the West Coast. Then unloaded off the trains and loaded onto the ships that then would head full steam ahead to Korea, and hopefully get there before the swarming down massed North Korean Army could push our Army down and down and further down and into the sea even.

To the adults across the country it was Pearl Harbor all over again. And so soon, too soon. How dare they! We will show them! And to my Mom and Dad also. And to the Moms and Dads of my best buddies whose Dads were Civil Service. But to the Moms and Dads of my best buddies whose Dads were Marine Officers, it was all that and so much more. There was plenty of shock and rage and fear to go around.

But unknown to us, the first loaded troop train was already coming out of Camp Lejeune as that first afternoon's newspapers were being delivered. Then later word swept Midway Park than an empty train was going into Camp Lejeune. So later that night all of us were lined up from the Main Gate for a mile along the road toward Jacksonville to watch the loaded train leave. But all we could see in the full darkness were the too brightly lighted passing faces in the windows of the troop cars, and the shadowy outlines of amphibious landing crafts and the heavy trucks and the artillery pieces on the flatcars. But we clapped and waved and hollered and cried anyway.

Early the next morning another loaded train came out. Since it was June and school was out, every kid who lived in Midway park was lined along the first mile toward Jacksonville. And most of the Moms were there also. But the Dads were at work on Base. As the first passenger car of Marines passed, the clapping and waving and hollering and crying began again. Since we were on a slight rise and the two lane road was not very wide and since the spur line was just on the other side of the road, the faces of the seated Marines in the windows seemed quite close. Their faces first showed the surprise that we were lined there to see them leave. And their faces showed the all the day before and the all of last night exhaustion of gathering gear and getting packed and getting loaded the all that they would need to fight a war. And now that they were finally pulling out of Camp Lejeune, their faces had begun to show the realization that now that their long trip had started, the end of their long trip would be Korea.

But I was so overwhelmed by the all that I was seeing and its meanings that I could not clap or wave or holler or cry. I could only watch each face in each window in each car as they passed. I carefully watched each face, and with each face, I heard the clickity clack of the wheels. Face clickity clack, face clickity clack, face clickity clack, car after car after car. Then suddenly the clickity clack of flatcars of amphibious landing crafts, then tanks clickity clack, then big trucks, then jeeps clickity clack, then artillery pieces clickity clack. This long train of many passenger cars of Marines, and many flatcars of their war equipment, going to Korea lickity split as fast as they could. By the time the last flatcar had passed, I could no longer stand. So I sat down and crossed my legs Indian style and rested my face on my palms, and carefully watched where the long troop train had passed, as I replayed in my mind its passing again and again. Yesterday, all of this Marines and their war gear and their equipment was the normal fun background to my normal kid world. Today what I had watched was the serious start of any war, all wars, everywhere, and the serious purpose for Marines and their war gear and equipment. But I still could not clap or wave or holler or cry.

During the next several days, the coming in of empty trains and the going out of loaded trains continued around the clock, and therefore quickly became the routine. And as with any routine, the crowds along the mile toward Jacksonville became smaller and smaller. Then it became mostly groups of boys like me and my best buddies. Then there were days when I was the only one who came to watch. But now I was waving at each face, face, face, face, face, because I thought they would want me to. And many waved back. Then one day my Dad came and stood beside me, and we watched and waved.

Then Dad said, Son, me and Mom are worried about you.

And I said, but Dad I have to be here.

And he said, well I know they appreciate your being here, but you don't have need to be here for every train.

And I said, but Dad they aren't going to get there before we are pushed down into the sea.

And he said, Son, there are plenty of other Army and Marine troops already in the Pacific, and they will get there in time so that doesn't happen.

So I thought about that.

Then Dad said, our Marines will be used later when we need an amphibious landing to surprise the North Koreans when and where they least expect it.

So I thought about that also.

Then during the next several days, the coming and going of the troop trains became fewer and fewer. Because the first assault Marines and their war gear were almost complete and on their way lickity split. Now their support Marines and their war gear started being sent to the nearby port at Morehead City by buses and flatbed trucks, to be loaded onto ships and then to go through the Panama Canal to Korea. Now all I had to do was to go behind my house in Midway Park and stand beside the road going to Swansboro and wave from there. But buses and flatbed trucks did not have the stunning urgency and the gripping drama that the troop trains had had.

Then in the fall of that year, I was in the Ninth Grade. I was in High School finally! And that in itself became a huge distraction. Because I could see the beginning of whiskers in the mirror. And because the girls in my class had begun to grow breasts. So I went out for the football team to impress them, and to impress myself also, but would up not impressing anyone.

And in the next several years the Korean War happened pretty much as Dad said it would. But in spite of everything that was going on in my High School life, I always made time to read the afternoon newspapers and to listen to the radio news broadcasts to keep up with how my first assault Marines from the troop trains were doing and where. Then later, when President Truman fired

General McArthur, I badly wanted to go to Washington and put my shoe in President Truman's ass. Because he had also stopped my Marines just when they had covered themselves in glory, and now had a roaring charging assault going, and were heading lickity split for Communist China itself. The few, the proud, the Marines.

Then, the next year, I left home and went to college, and that certainly was a world apart from anything in my earlier world for sure. Then later still, when I had gotten a job and had begun to crisscross the South on business, I had almost completely separated myself from my earlier world. Then with the pressures and responsibilities that happen to all of us, the years began to pass fast then faster still. The usual blurry kaleidoscope of years of happiness and sadness and success and failure.

But all along, I still had the passion that I had as that kid. It is just that after such a long journey it has become frayed a bit and faded a bit around the edges. So I do not bring out my passion for others to see very often anymore. Because it upsets them, and troubles them, and therefore makes me suspect. So now my passion just as soon stay inside of me where it is welcome and warm and comfortable.

And other Wars had come and gone also. Each completely consuming our attention for their time of importance. Until, now the Korean War seems remote and long ago, and vague history in a book on a dusty shelf. Then one day last week, I came out of a grocery store and started to walk to a car that was parked a little past where everyone else had parked. There was a man who was a few steps ahead of me, going from left to right, and about to cross in front of me, going to his car that was parked beside mine. I looked and saw that he had a few more gray hairs and wrinkles than I have and therefore was several years older than me, just as all of us make quick judgments about people as we pass them. Then I looked at the rear window of his car and saw that there was a large very worn Marine Corps emblem there. So as he crossed in front of me, and without thinking, I said in a low throaty growl of pride, "Marine!" and he answered in the same low throaty growl of pride, "Semper Fi!" Then as we were about to get into our cars, we looked at each other again and waved. Then he drove on to the parking lot exit. And that was it. That was all of it.

But as I turned the ignition key to my car, suddenly in a staggering rush from remote long ago, I saw the kid that was me standing on the rise across from Camp Lejeune Main Gate watching a loaded troop train leaving for Korea. And suddenly also, I knew that the old Marine was also having his own staggering rush from the remote long ago, as he was now pulling out into the traffic, of his forlornly looking out of the troop train passenger car window, and then seeing a lone kid on the rise across from the Camp Lejeune Main Gate waving at him, the day he left for Korea.

And I know also that both of us were hearing the clickity click clickity clack of the rails of way back then. That we both were reliving the full drama and pride and fear of it all. That we both, kid and young Marine, were suddenly again caught in that moment in history, that neither of us wanted, that neither of us fully understood, that neither of us could avoid. That both of us, each in our own way, were going to war again. Me to live the passion of it.

208

Him to live the horror of it.

www.ingramcontent.com/pod-product-compliance
Lightning Source LLC
Chambersburg PA
CBHW050529260626
47157CB00004B/1531